Tom Hall

The Little Lady, Some Other People, and Myself

Tom Hall

The Little Lady, Some Other People, and Myself

ISBN/EAN: 9783337120252

Printed in Europe, USA, Canada, Australia, Japan

Cover: Foto ©Andreas Hilbeck / pixelio.de

More available books at **www.hansebooks.com**

THE LITTLE LADY.

The Little Lady, Some Other People and Myself.

BY

TOM HALL,

Author of

" When Love Laughs," "When Hearts Are Trumps," etc.

New York.

E. R. Herrick & Company.

70 Fifth Avenue.

WEED-PARSONS PRINTING COMPANY,
PRINTERS AND ELECTROTYPERS,
ALBANY, N. Y.

TO MY CHILDREN.

TABLE OF CONTENTS.

[9]

A Boy's Fads

I BOUGHT him rattles as much for my own pleasure as his. It was a delight to me to see the little mite of humanity make a stir in the world. It was the same with his playthings. In fact, I often caught myself lamenting the fact that they did not have such playthings when I was a boy.

Presently, however, I discovered that he had been born with the human failing of "wanting things." It was brought very forcibly to my attention by a demand from him for a box of tools. I did not like the idea of tools. And it was about time to teach him that he could not have everything he wanted, so I went over to a friend older and much wiser than myself and held a consultation.

"Get him the tools," said my friend. "He has got to take his chances of getting hurt all through life, and as for teaching him that he can't have everything he wants, he has got to learn that for himself." He got the tools. Then it soon became apparent that his desires were a continuous performance.

After the tools, he wanted a cat to hunt rats with, and after the cat a dog to hunt cats with. Then he got in turn, a bicycle, skates, and a bob-sled. During the next summer he became a member of a baseball team, and concurrent with baseball came desires for chickens, white mice and rabbits. The next summer it was fishing and swimming, and the autumn succeeding it was football. That winter it was hunting, and I had to buy him a gun, although his mother protested, and to this day will not go to the garret alone where it is kept, for fear it will go off. I only wish it would go off — and stay.

About this time I had fond hopes for his future career, and began planning day dreams such as some years before I had had concerning myself. But it seemed more reasonable to dream of great things for him. He would be able to benefit by my advice, and that would be a great help. I had never followed my father's advice, but that was because he did not know nearly so much as I did. But it is plain to anyone that I know more than my boy does. So I asked him one day what he would like to be when he became a man.

"A policeman," said he promptly.

I went over to my wise old friend for consolation. He merely laughed at me.

"To-morrow, or a month hence," said he, "he will want to be a fireman; then a street car driver. After that a postman and railroad engineer. Later he will think seriously of becoming a cowboy and slayer of Indians. He will also plan to become a bareback rider in a circus, and he will rig up a trapeze in your back yard."

"How long will this last?" I asked.

"Oh, let me see," the old man replied, "I think until he begins to collect stamps. Yes, and after stamps will come birds' eggs, autographs, minerals and curiosities."

"And after that?" I asked, dolefully

"After that will come lighter exercise, tennis and horseback riding. Then will come music, and heaven protect you from the cornet. Try to steer him toward the flute or violin. The sounds of these may be more or less deadened, and you can make him practice in the barn. With the desire to make pleasant sounds will come the desire for girls. Yes, girls will come at last, and they are a fad which we never get over. Don't be worried, however. He will not want to get married right off. It will be after college and after a few love affairs. And the chances are that he will marry the right girl, even if she is not the girl you and your wife have picked out."

"Well, that will end the fads, anyway," I interjected.

"Not at all," said my old friend. "After that will come children. You're only a boy enjoying the latest of your fads yourself."

I suppose the old man is right. But I have one thing to look forward to. When that boy of mine is grown up and has children of his own, won't I have fun watching him bring them up? Oh, the trouble he'll have! But, confound it, come to think about it they'll be my grandchildren and another fad of my own.

I WEED IN THE GARDEN.

THE weeds grow in our garden with tropical luxuriance. We'd (grab the pun before it gets away, it belongs to you) rather they wouldn't, but they grow right along just the same. Indeed, my wife expects to wear weeds when I die. She says I won't leave enough of an estate to buy clothes with. Well, I wouldn't get red-headed about the weeds if they would only be neighborly with the vegetables in our garden; but they won't — not even with the flowers. So we determined to get rid of them. That was two months ago. My wife called her friend Puss (a pretty girl) into consultation, and the plan adopted by a vote of two to one (I voting in the negative) was for me to pull the weeds out with my delicate, yet aristocratic hands. I filed a protest, but eventually promised to do the weeding when I got around to it.

I did not get around to it until yesterday. The little lady and Puss went out for an extended trip on their wheels, and as I was in my lordliest humor, I concluded to give them a surprise when they got back by having the garden nicely weeded for them. So I got a hoe and a rake and a scythe and a pick-axe and went to work. You should have seen those weeds disappear before my victorious onslaught. There was one immensely tall and thick weed that I took a keen delight in annihilating. It was such a large, audacious weed that I called it the Boss (T)weed of my garden. I must confess that I had some misgivings about some of the plants I weeded out. When I got through, the only things left standing were the tomato plants and the woodshed. I know tomato plants from their resemblance to geraniums.

It was not until the ladies came home, however, that I discovered that I had weeded out all the vegetables save the aforesaid tomato plants, and half of the flowers. And among the flowers that I destroyed were, I regret to say, my wife's favorite double poppies (query: Is a "double poppy" the father of twins?) and some Marshal O'Neil and Glory de Dungeon roses. The most precious product that I destroyed, however, was my wife's great bunch of sunflowers. Too late I learned that my Boss (T)weed was that particular kind of a flower. But there is one glorious thing about it.   Those women will not ask me to weed the garden again. Little by little I am eliminating work from my life; but the little lady says I am doing it on the same plan as I weeded the garden.

MY PEAR TREES.

I DIDN'T believe a lot of rustics would have the nerve to fool with a real city man, when I came here to live in Hayville. I told them a few adventures of mine on the Bowery, and how I had once answered back a policeman (in the ante-Roosevelt era), and I thought I had scared the whole crowd. My ultimate object, in all this, was to keep the villagers away from the pear trees in the lot I had rented and which surrounded the house wherein I intended to live forevermore. As the days moved carelessly by I smiled a knowing smile, and became more and more convinced that my big bluff about that Broadway policeman and my hints about man-traps, shot-guns, poison and bloodhounds had had their effect. And so it came to pass that I vaunted me in the public post-office (which is just outside the private post-office, where the postmaster and his family read the mail before they give it out) about my success, and derided the inhabitants of the whole county.

"Now, Meester," said the justice of the peace, in reply, "you must remember that your pears weren't fit to eat till to-day. Give 'em time."

I told him that I would be in my house the next day and would give 'em buckshot, instead of time, if they ever stole any of my pears.

Well, I would if they ever did. But the fact of the matter is, I haven't any pears. All of mine were stolen that same evening, before I moved in. I found a pitchfork under one of the trees, that had evidently been used for the purpose of pulling down some of the high-flying pears, and I awaited with delight the appearance of the owner. Who should the owner prove to be but that same old justice of the peace! He came around with the most innocent expression on his face imaginable, and said that the same crowd that stole my pears had stolen his pitchfork, and that he wanted to recover his property. I am really beginning to wish I were back among the dear old honest, simple, confidence men of New York.

COASTING IN HERKIMER COUNTY.

I USED to like to coast when I lived in St. Louis years ago. We boys used to catch the snow in bed sheets and carry it over to a hill, throw it on and get in a coast or two before it melted. I'm living now in Herkimer county and I'm learning what snow, ice, north winds and coasting really are.

The other day a young gentleman who saws my wood for me invited me to go coasting with him. I gladly assented, forgetting for the nonce that we are about two thousand feet above tide water at Troy. Nor did I take into consideration the fact that the descent in any direction from my home averages about four hundred feet to the mile for several miles. So I sat on the "Bob" or "Robert" sleigh, as I suppose it should be called, with satisfaction and calm. A moment later we started.

When I recovered consciousness I discovered that we were sailing through the universe at the rate of twenty miles a minute. On either side there seemed to be a white mist which I soon found to be snow clad hills and farms. We passed by them so quickly that the eye would get a sort of kaleidoscopic view only, and the roof of one farmhouse would appear to be attached to the body of another a mile or more away.

"Lie down," shouted my Jehu. I did so, and we shot under a cow that was crossing the road. We went by her, or under her rather, so quickly that she did not even notice us. It was the same with a wagon and a four-horse team. We went under the wagon and between the horses so quickly that we were invisble, although I distinctly heard the driver remark, "Gosh! thought I heard somethin' swish!" Our next adventure was a trifle more exciting. The road made a turn at the foot of a hill, and at the turn stood a frame house. Our sleigh was going at such a rate that, of course, it jumped clear of the hill. We went in at a second-story window at the front of the house and came out at another at the back. A woman was sitting in the room we traversed rocking a baby. I lifted my hat to apologize for our rudeness, but the apology was made to a young lady a mile further on, who did not seem to understand.

I do not know exactly when we passed Troy, Albany and Peekskill, but in the course of time, much to my wonder, we came to a full stop.

"Well, Mister," said the young man, "How's that for a three-mile slide? Here we are in Middleville."

"Young man," I answered, solemnly. "Don't try to deceive one so old in the ways of this wicked world. This may look like Middleville and I acknowledge that it smells like it. But nevertheless it is and must be Harlem. Show me the way to the nearest station of the Sixth Avenue L, if you please."

AN ANNOYING COMPATIBILITY OF TEMPER.

Breathes there a man, and he is wed,
Who never to himself has said:
"I wish, by Jingo, I was dead?"

WHEN I married it was my luck to get a
woman with the sweetest disposition
that ever smoothed the wrinkles out of the
brow of care. The result is that I am lazy,
shiftless, good for-nothing; unknown to
fame and in debt to the grocer. In fact I
am the kind of a man who shuffles around
with his hands in his pockets and an old
corn-cob pipe sticking out of the northeast
corner of his mouth, too durned happy and
contented to get out of the way of a runa-
way team if it happens to be coming in my
direction.

When I see a rich man, a successful man,
or a famous man, I say to myself: "Now
that fellow had the luck to get a nagging
wife. He had to hustle just to keep his
mind from his misery." Talk about genius.
It's all rot. It's a nagging wife that does
the business every time. I could instance a

number of cases, but I don't want to give the poor, suffering great men of my country away.

If I had only been provided with a wife who would call me an infernal ass about 'steen times a day, pitch my pipes and to-bacco into the street, make me comb my hair and waylay me with a rolling pin every time I came back from a political or other discussion at the post-office, I might in time amount to something. As it is, look at me, or rather look the other way.

When I do occasionally take pen in hand and do a little work my wife insists that the product is the best literature ever furnished to the helpless American public. Every time I write anything she assures me that it is the best thing I ever wrote, and one time she even insisted that my penmanship was improving. I tried to get her to change the formula once by copying out the multiplication table and offering it to her as a specimen of may burning genius. But she didn't see the joke at all. On the contrary, she earnestly declared that it was far better than anything I had ever written before.

And so it goes with everything else. She is just as well contented with candles as electric lights, with calico as silk, and with pebble as diamonds — although I will admit that she hasn't had much experience with diamonds yet. I have begged her on my knees to get mad at me and find fault with me. I have pointed out to her what I might become if she would only act as other men's wives do. But she is incorrigible. I have convinced her of the fact that it is all her fault that I amount to nothing. She meekly acknowledges the error of her ways and says she cannot help it.

Not long ago I tried to startle her into making some kind of a protest at a more than usually insane proposition of mine. I went home in a pretended hurry one day and told her to pack up immediately, as I intended starting for the North Pole and taking her and the baby along with me.

She was delighted, and began packing up at once. And that night when she was putting the baby to bed I overheard her saying to our future President:

"Would 'im's blessed heart like to play with the little icebergs?" To which the baby replied:

"Yeth, ma'am, wif tunnin' little baby icebergs."

The next morning I informed her that I

had abruptly changed my plans, and that I intended to start for the equator instead.

"Oh," said she, "that will be ever so much more delightful. And it won't cost nearly as much for clothes and food; and you, poor, dear boy, you won't have to work nearly so hard, will you?"

I give it up.

What are you going to do with a woman like that?

MY EXPERIENCE AS AN INSTRUCTOR IN BUSINESS.

I AWOKE one morning last week in an unusually good humor, and, after a brain food breakfast, prepared for a morning stroll in order to commune with Nature. Unfortunately for my projected stroll, I discovered that every hat I owned was several sizes too small for me, on that particular morning, and I was compelled *ex necessitate*, as we used to say in Rome, to loaf around the house and make myself disagreeable to the women folks. The fact is that I had made a couple of dollars on the previous day and had said something so funny that it made Somebody laugh. I have since tried to find out from Somebody what it was that I said, but he has forgotten. I have also blown in the couple of dollars. My hats fit better now, thank you.

I had to have a victim on this particular morning, however, and (just as any other man would do under the circumstances) I picked out the most available one — my wife. I determined that I would give her a lesson in business methods. She is so young she does not have to lie about her age, and every time she transacts any business she is imposed upon — as soon as I find it out. Myself am a business man from away back. I have never made a cent in a business transaction yet, but I have had lots of experience. And if experience does not make a business man, what does?

On this particular morning the rag man came, and I scented my opportunity (and him) from afar. The little lady brought forth a bag of rags that she had been saving up and proceeded to bargain. I took a cup of strong tea, lit a ten-cent cigar, and got my kinetic energy going like a buzz saw.

"How many pounds?" asked the little lady, anxiously.

"Just fifteen pounds," answered the rag man, "hefting" the bag, as they say in the rural districts.

"Weigh it," said I, in my most authoritative manner. The rag man pulled a pair of battered scales from his hip pocket, hooked them to the bag quite silently, and exhibited

the result. The scales showed just fifteen
pounds.

"What a splendid guess!" exclaimed the
little lady, enthusiastically.

"How much will you take for the scales?"
I growled in my most cynical manner.

Well, after some further bargaining and
after throwing in three cents to boot (the
rags went at a cent a pound), the little lady
emerged from the *melée* with a sauce pan
that the rag man said was cheap at twenty
cents. After this I took the little lady into
my study and read aloud to her eight chap-
ters from a book on domestic economy.
Then I borrowed a hat from a large man
who lives across the street and took the little
lady and the sauce pan she had just acquired
in barter and trade, up to the village store.
The storekeeper said he would be glad to
sell us one just like it (only cleaner) for ten
cents. I smiled in triumph. But the little
lady's lips quivered, and I was afraid she
was going to cry right then and there.
After we got home I went into my study
and spent the rest of the day luxuriating in
the thought of my cleverness.

After supper, however, the little lady
came to me, kissed me on my talented fore-
head and spake thus:

"My dear, I know I was very foolish, and I won't do so any more. I was only trying to help along the best I could. I spent hours getting those old things together just so I could add a little something to our store without spending your hard-earned money every time. But I'll be more sensible the next time."

Then I wanted to take an evening stroll and think some more. But, do you know, every one of my hats had grown so big that the gentle evening zephyrs blew them away in succession before I could get from the front door to the gate!

I wish somebody would invent an adjustable hat. I want one badly.

WHY I WANT TO MEET MARK TWAIN ON A DARK, LONELY ROAD AT MIDNIGHT— I BEING ARMED TO THE TEETH AND HE DEFENSELESS.

BLOOD! REVENGE! !
Many innocent people will remember
an article upon railway travel written by
one Mark Twain, and published some time
ago in an influential magazine. In it he
suggested a plan by which the passenger
could obtain courtesy and other things from
the railway officials with whom he was
thrown in contact on his wanderings. The
plan was simplicity itself. It was merely to
claim an acquaintance with one of the high
officials of the road and demand something

better than "A 1" in the matter of treatment. The plan struck me as being a good one. Mark said he used it himself with unfailing success, and ever since I heard the story of the "Jumping Frog" I have believed that it would be utterly impossible for Mark to tell a lie. Consequently I determined to use it on the first possible occasion.

Now, it happens that I do not travel much; but a short time ago business took me from New York to Chicago. When I purchased my ticket at the Grand Central Station I murmured these magic words to the clerk: "I am a warm personal friend of Mr. Depew's." The clerk smiled but said nothing. However, the smile was encouraging at a time when I needed encouragement. The fact is I'm not much of a liar myself. Any of my friends will tell you that. I was just a trifle disappointed though. I had expected a considerable reduction in the rate if not a pass from that ticket seller. And the fellow not only gave me the exact change, but he worked off a counterfeit half dollar on me! "Perhaps he thinks I'm so rich I won't notice a mere half dollar," I reasoned with myself. "No doubt all Mr. Depew's warm personal friends are rich." I passed on to the seller of the sleeping car tickets, undismayed.

"A lower berth for Chicago," said I.

"Lower berths all sold, sir. Have an upper?"

"But, my good man," I suggested, "Mr. W. Seward Webb, 'Sew' as I call him, is a first cousin of mine."

"Oh! I meet lots of Mr. Webb's cousins," said the clerk. "In fact he has issued orders disowning all his cousins, male and female." I left the window in high dudgeon. I don't know what "dudgeon" is, but I have often heard the expression.

I made my way to the Chicago sleeper. The porter asked for my ticket, but I told him I would buy one from the conductor.

"I'm a warm personal friend and business associate of Depew's," said I, *sotto voce*.

(There's another term I wot not of, except that it sounds well.)

"You're another of them, are you?" said the porter with a chuckle and giving me a dig in the ribs. "Oh, I meet lots of them." But he let me pass and I took a seat in the smoking compartment.

There were two gentlemen in the smoking compartment, and I dropped into conversation with them. I like my little joke and I told them of my adventure with the ticket sellers and the porter, and bade them watch me work the sleeping car conductor. They were greatly amused, and one of them said there was nothing he liked better than a good joke. They promised to stay and see the fun.

Eventually the train started and the sleeping car conductor made his appearance. My two companions preserved a dignified silence. I was fearfully afraid they would grin ahead of time and thus give me away, but they behaved admirably. They acted as though they had never spoken a word to me in their lives.

"A lower berth to Chicago," said I, nonchalantly.

"Lower berths all gone sir — one upper left. Will you have that?"

"Certainly not," I answered with some asperity. "I am an intimate friend and business associate of Dr. Depew's. If I do not get a lower berth on this train he shall most certainly hear of it."

"I am very sorry —" began the conductor. But I did not let him proceed. I saw that I was making an impression and I determined to strike while the iron was hot.

"Moreover, I am the favorite first cousin

of Mr. W. Seward Webb, and he shall hear of it also."

"You know them?" exclaimed the conductor in blank amazement.

"Know them?" said I. "Why we were boys together. They're both in Europe now, but when they get back you'll hear from me."

"Why — why — this is Dr. Depew," said the conductor, pointing to one of the gentlemen in the smoking compartment, "and this is Mr. Webb." The two gentlemen began laughing uproariously.

I am a man of action and there was but one thing to do. I flung my bag through the window of the flying train and jumped out after it.

But the worst I have not told to you.

I have since learned that Depew and Webb were actually in Europe at the time. The conductor had simply called my bluff and made a bigger one.

But if ever I meet Mark Twain, under the circumstances enumerated above, pray for him!

My Plaque.

I COMMITTED it several years ago, and this is my confession. It is also the exposition of the cruel and unusual punishment that has been visited upon a free-born American citizen in utter defiance of the Constitution. And it is a mild hint to Congress to give me some redress.

I will preface my remarks by saying that I could not draw a right line with a ruler.

My professor of drawing at West Point once looked over my shoulder while I was endeavoring to depict a scene from Nature with a crayon. Then, like Washington at Monmouth, he uttered an oath for the first time in his life. But he never looked at any of my work again. If he had he would never have permitted me to graduate.

It was shortly after I was married that it occurred, and my wife and I had a young lady friend (those last two words sound too New Yorky to be literature, but they will have to go) who used oil colors very deftly. I determined to learn. She was very kind and appeared interested in me, as it were, and she started me copying a donkey's head on a plaque. I traced in the outlines that same day, and she promised to come over and start me with the colors the next day. On the morrow, however, it rained pitchforks and bayonets, and she signaled from her house that she could not come over. Now I have an impatient temperament and a foolish desire to go ahead and do things whether I know how to do them or not. I spread some assorted colors on my palette, grabbed a handful of brushes and waded in. I was going to say that before the day was over I waded in oil up to my knees. It was in reality down to my knees, for I saved enough of my trousers to make a very serviceable pen-wiper. My coat and vest I gave to the poor. The poor gave it to the rag man.

But I completed my plaque just the same, and I hung it on the wall to be admired. That evening my friend Jones came in to play a game of chess. He doesn't mind the weather, and he likes my tobacco.

"Jones, old boy," I said to him, pointing to my plaque, "what do you think of that for an Old Master?" Jones took a squint.

"One of your ancestors?" he inquired.

Fortunately I know that Jones is nearsighted.

The next day my little preceptress came over to give her lesson. She took one look at my completed product, and then she left the room and sought my wife. Then those two fool women went out to the barn and had hysterics. I felt that they were weeping, and followed later to console them, though I knew not the reason of their sorrow. What do you suppose they were doing? They were laughing. They were both red in the face, and they had taken off their belts for safety. As I tried to make my sneak and study the matter over I heard my preceptress say to my wife, "What shall I say to him? I don't want to hurt his feelings, but just look at it! One ear is eight inches higher than the other. One eye is green and the other purple. And the prominent nostril looks like the Mammoth Cave." That made me mad. I took that plaque down and went over to see Mrs. Smith, a nice, quiet, appreciative little woman who doesn't know too derned much about art. I made her a present of it, and then I did the offended dignity act until those two women were heartily ashamed of themselves.

But they were right. I have seen a great many paintings since then and have studied them carefully. I have met many artists and talked with them. I have also met many asses in real life. And a day came when I wanted to take that infernal plaque and tear it limb from limb. But nice, quiet, appreciative Mrs. Smith wouldn't let me have it. To her it was a *chef d'œuvre*, and a whole menu in French besides. I ground my teeth and accepted my fate as stoically as I could.

Well, the Smiths had a fire the other night. Their house was burned to the ground. I love them, but I got out of bed and went to that fire with all the kerosene in the house, determined to help it along all I could. When I arrived at the scene of the conflagration (as the young newspaper reporter says) Mrs. Smith fell into my arms.

"Oh, Mr. Hall," she cried, "we have lost almost everything, but we have saved your plaque."

That settled it. Now, when the twilight falls, and there is in the sky that "clear obscure"

> "Which follows the decline of day
> As twilight melts beneath the moon away."

I go out to the uttermost confines of our two-acre lot and softly swear. Then I spend an hour regaining my peace of mind. After which I say my prayers, retire, and endeavor not to dream of that confounded plaque.

My Summer in a Chicken-Coop.

MY SUMMER IN A CHICKEN-COOP.

TO amuse the little lady and the youngsters I bought six hens and a rooster. Then I had a chicken-coop erected and the fowls incarcerated. Life in the country is rather dull for the little lady. She is more accustomed to the buzz, hum, and whirr of the wilds of New York. She thought she would like to hunt for eggs, and the youngster assured me he would like to play with "little chick-chicks." When he said so I mentally ejaculated, "Heaven help the chick-chicks!"

But the hens and the rooster were bought and delivered about sundown and each of them named within an hour. The next morning I arose and ascended to my study in the attic with the firm determination of writing, from "morn till noon," a poem that would bring me in at least ten dollars and a sketch that would sell in the market for five; also of writing, "from noon till dewy eve," a short story that would easily sell anywhere for twenty-five units of the necessary. Total, forty dollars. I had no sooner seated myself at my desk, however, and got mine eye into a fine frenzy rolling, than I heard a scream and the little lady rushed in to inform me that "Grace" had escaped from the coop and was out in the garden. I dopped my prose and poetry and adopted grim-visaged war. In other words, I went out into the garden and took command.

On the right I stationed my wife, on the left our hired girl and in the center the youngster. I myself remained in the rear as commander-in-chief and reserve. I will not detail the many evolutions of that campaign. I am too modest to dwell upon the excellence of my strategy. Suffice it to say that my brave troops eventually succeeded in reaching their objective, and by noon the next day Grace surrendered at discretion and was cooped up where we wanted her. We changed her name then to Maud, because she came out in the garden. We had originally named her Grace because she was the prettiest and the whitest of our hens, and we knew of a young lady of that name who was as pretty and white as a young girl can be, which is saying a great deal.

After that we had many other experiences. The little lady had lots of fun hunting for eggs, but she usually found that her hens had laid them up at the store, and that the proprietor would not surrender them without the passing of coin. I did not have to spend my whole summer in a chicken-coop, however. As the spring wore on I had more experiences. My rooster had some fighting blood in him and was much prized by several of our villagers. He disappeared mysteriously. Two of my hens were killed by rats and two died. What the latter couple died of I really cannot say. Every farmer within ten miles has assigned a different disease as the cause. I have made a combination of the names of these diseases and consider it the cause of their demise; but it is too long to repeat in one breath or get into one sentence. Maud, true to her instinct, again came out into our garden and then went into a neighbor's. I have a strong suspicion that she is now in that neighbor's chicken-coop, but as he and I are the very best of friends I do not like to say anything. At present I have one hen left, and I am wondering.

4

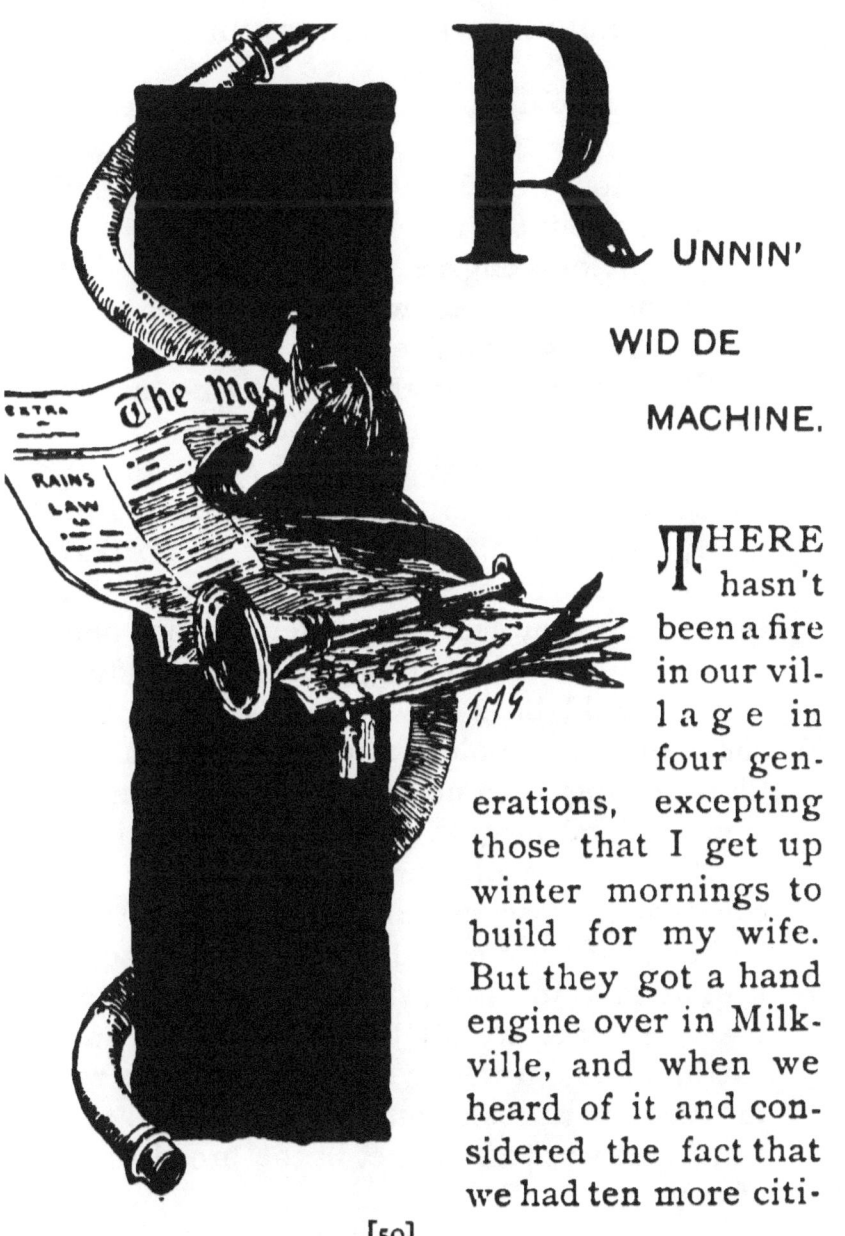

R

UNNIN'

WID DE

MACHINE.

THERE hasn't been a fire in our village in four generations, excepting those that I get up winter mornings to build for my wife. But they got a hand engine over in Milkville, and when we heard of it and considered the fact that we had ten more citizens and an old maid more than they had in Milkville, we gritted our teeth, determined that we, too, would have an engine, and that we would paint it red.

We got our engine. We purchased our uniforms. And then we waited for a fire.

But there was no fire.

When we first bought our engine (never mind the grammar, I am speaking in the popular phraseology of the day) our insurance rates were promptly reduced. But later, when developments came to the capacious ears of the insurance agents, the rates were doubled. The fact is every one in town got to wishing that somebody's house would burn down, just so we could show what we could do with our machine. This feeling became so intense that after a while (and after a number of ingenious combustible contrivances had been discovered in close proximity to houses that looked as if they would make a picturesque fire) no man in the town spoke to any other man. In fact we all bought shotguns and patrolled our premises during the night, reluctantly permitting our wives to do all the work that was to be done, in the broad light of day.

I do not know what would have happened

if a little relief had not come from Curd
Corners, seven miles away.   One of their
village wise men got mad at his wife because she could not make green wood burn
in their cook stove and endeavored to show
her how, with the contents of a kerosene
lamp.

They called us up by telephone and we re-
sponded like "heroes," as they say in South
Africa.   Every man put on his best uniform
and   polished   up   his   helmet   before   we
started.   I even went so far as to turn my
cuffs, for I vowed that if I had to die fighting the fierce flames I would die like a gentleman.   Then we started for Curd Corners.
You should have heard the women and children cheer us as we raced out of town.

But oh, what a long seven miles that was
to Curd Corners!   I do not believe we
would have ever arrived at our destination
if it had not been for Bill Smith.   He is our
assistant   foreman   and   runs   the   village
saloon.   Fortunately he brought the saloon
along with him.   He had most of it wrapped
up in old copies of the Raines Law.   This
to deceive the women and children.

Well, we got to Curd Corners in the course
of several hours and you should have heard
the Curd Cornerites yell.   They were try-

ing at the same time to save the Methodist church, and they were delighted. We dashed up to a well with a wild hurrah. But we didn't pump any water. The fact of the matter was, we had forgotten to bring along the pipe that you drop down into the well. I don't know what its name is, although I tried to catch it while our foreman was cussing at us.

The mean part of it was, however, that the Curd Cornerites were ungentlemanly enough to jeer at us, and suggest that we turn to and help in the bucket lines. But we wouldn't do anything so far beneath our dignity as that. We went silently home.

We have since disbanded our company and have sold our machine to the people of Curd Corners.

DISCIPLINING A SMALL BOY.

MOST of the fathers in the land will understand just what I am going to say, merely from the title of this sketch. They need not listen to my tale of woe unless they wish to. This is an appeal for sympathy, but it is made to those who do not understand the situation.

The boy is two and a half years old. According to the family Bible I am thirty-three, but, after an analytical study of my symptoms, I am convinced that in the last two years and a half I have jumped to a hundred and thirty-three years of age and more of experience.

When the youngster made us his first bow, I went immediately to the seller of tomes and bought a copy of Herbert Spencer's "Education." Of this I made a study, was much impressed, and with a whack of my fist on the table declared that our boy should never be spanked. Since then I have often wondered if Herbert ever had any children.

But Herbert was not our only guide, philosopher and friend (?). Our boy had (besides his parents) grandmothers, great-grandmothers, five hundred thousand aunts and one million cousins. One of the aunts was a kindergarten sharp. She declared imperatively that he ought not to have anything to play with, for two years, but a red ball. It was hard to hear this, but we supposed she ought to know. It brought a bit of a swear word from me, that ultimatum did, and my wife had a cry over it. The fact is we had been looking forward to the day when his plump little fist would grasp a rattle and shake it until his eyes danced with joy. He got the rattle, and he got more. In fact large areas of our dwelling look like a toy shop. I suppose he should have had nothing but the red ball; but we are human.

Then we determined to run that boy ourselves, and we removed ourselves far, far away from anything in the shape of a relative. It was then that we discovered that an occasional spanking was an absolute necessity and a tonic as well. I have given

Herbert's book to a new father and am enjoying the fun he is having with it. At the same time it was hard to do the spanking, and I devoutly thank heaven that I have finally finessed his mother into doing most of it.

We tried other disciplinary methods, however. One of our first was to make him stand in a corner, with his face to the wall. This worked beautifully for a month or so. Then he got to going into the corner of his own accord and grinning at us, with one eye slanted in our direction to see if we appreciated the joke. We went back to spanking. Later in his career he adopted the boyish habit of running away. We tried picketing him out to a tree. It worked all right as long as he thought he was playing horse. But when he discovered the trick that had been played on him he uttered such a pitiful yell that his mother, with a worried brow and a determined contraction of the dimple in her chin, went out and freed him. Ten minutes later I saw her chasing up the street after him, her arms covered with dough and her hair on anything but straight. She found him at the post-office reciting to the men who most do congregate in such places a poem about a certain "Fat Man of Bombay."

Our last resource failed us not long ago. We tried putting him to bed. But it did not worry him a little bit. He amused himself learning to whistle and made rapid progress. But I have made up my mind what to do. I am going to get the government to give me a detail of a couple of army officers to take charge of his discipline. To take some of the strain from them I am going to hire four tutors from assorted colleges; and to take some of the strain from their nervous systems I am also going to hire eight trained nurses. Who is to help the nurses I have not figured out yet, but I may be able to do so later. I sincerely hope that none of these fourteen disciplinarians have heard of him. There he is now in the middle of the street. He has stopped a hay wagon and is standing in front of the horses saying, "Nice, whoa." The man who is driving is cussing under his breath; I can tell by the expression on his face. But he will have to wait till I get through with this before I go out and drag that boy away.

However, I have hopes of this last scheme. But if it does not work, will some kind friend, who is older and wiser than myself, please tell me what to do?

MY TOMATO PLANTS.

AFTER I had weeded my garden there was nothing left of it but three tomato plants, and rather sickly looking ones they were, too. But I was proud of them never-theless, for I had both planted them and spared them. The more they did not flourish the more I called attenticn to their good qualities, until they became a joke in the neighborhood and the subject of many a jest between my wife and pretty Puss. The more they joked me, however, the more I loved my plants, and I stood by them loyally.

One morning, to my great delight, I found the green vines bearing little green toma-toes, and a proud man I was. I went among my neighbors and told thereof, and to my unspeakable delight I found that my plants were the only ones in town that had begun to bear. Most of the others hadn't blos-comed yet. In fact I had not noticed mine blossom, but then I am not a very noticeable man (I have a dim suspicion that I have not said what I mean).

My tomatoes created quite a furore in

town, you may be sure, and most of my friends and all of my enemies came down to see them. And as they went away they laughed, and even while they looked at them many of them had the audacity to grin. I do not see the point of the joke yet, although I suppose there was one. But the fact was that those little green tomatoes didn't belong to my vines at all. The girls had sent South for them and had tied them on with green string.

I will get even with those women some day — that is, I will get even with Puss. I am even with my wife. I got even with her for many subsequent wrongs when I married her.

EVERY one knows that I am modest. Perhaps the great, wide world is not aware, however, of the fact that I am bashful as well. I do not like to put myself forward publicly before either large or small audiences. This peculiarity, together with an aversion to killing ducks, will eventually prevent my becoming President of the United States. However, let that pass. I have made up my mind to it, and there is no need for consolation. Hank Clay, Dan Webster, Jim Blaine and I will seek out a quiet spot somewhere in the great unknown and play a consolation game of whist until the last trump is turned.

But — does it not seem to you that I am diverging from the original subject of this sketch?

To return to it, therefore, I will say that we (the little lady and myself) were invited to an evening's amusement at the Blakes'. The Blakes are nice people who make you dress up and go out somewhere on cold, chilly evenings when you would much prefer to be burning the soles off your socks before your own grate fire. On account of my extreme bashfulness I am usually an incubus on such occasions. I am always saying something I ought not to, or doing something at the wrong time. Latterly I have hit upon the plan of saying and doing nothing. But this does not satisfy the little lady. She says it makes people wonder how she ever came to marry such a perfect fool as I am. She does not want them to wonder at it. She would much prefer that I should appear brilliant to the neighbors, dunce though I may be at home. At any rate she made me promise to make a stab at trying to pretend I was brilliant, and that evening she made me promise to do everything I was asked to do, and take part in all the festivities of the occasion. She was sorry afterward. But I did the best I could, as you shall see.

Well there was a fair, pale young girl from the city at the Blakes' that evening. She had received her education abroad and thumped the piano with both hands. She also spoke French without consulting the dictionary ever and anon, and was an all-round wonder. I was sitting on a fauteuil trying to look as graceful as possible under the circumstances, when the fair, pale young girl swung herself around the orbit of the piano stool and asked me if I wouldn't sing. Now I can't sing. That's the plain statement of the case. When I was at school the music teacher used to ask me with tears in his eyes not even to try. I don't know one tune from another, with the exception of "Old Hundred," and I only know that because it is so short. Naturally I was just going to decline when I thought of my promise to the little lady. I wouldn't break a promise to her for anything in this world.

"With pleasure," I answered the fair, pale young girl, and stepped briskly to her side. They told me afterward that the little lady

fainted when I did this. A woman always
knows when to faint.

"Do you read at sight ?" asked the fair,
pale young girl.

"Entirely by sight," I answered, wondering if there were people who read with their
ears.

"I am so glad," she
lisped, "I have here an
aria that I brought with
me from abroad. It is for
a baritone voice and I am
sure it will please you.
Let's begin at once."

With that she began
playing. Now I wasn't
fool enough to begin
singing right off. I
knew that there is al-
ways a little salute, as
one might say, on the
piano, before the singer
begins. I also knew that
you sing up or down
according as the notes
run up or down on the
telegraph wires with
which they print music. I knew, moreover,
that the singer begins when the pianist

commences to play "thump — thump, thump, — thump — thump, thump, etc." So when she played in that sort of a way I began, and I sang right through to the end. I would have been singing yet if she hadn't stopped playing, for I got so tangled up in that Sahara of notes, telegraph poles and wires that I had no idea where I was at. I did not get very much applause. And the fair, pale young girl went out of the room and had hysterics right alongside of my fainting wife. The rest of the women went to take care of her, and the men looked glum. I will say that Blake did his duty as a host, though. He said I had a tremendously strong voice. And I think he must be right, for they heard it up at the post-office, thought it was an alarm of fire and turned out with Old Red No. 1 and a gallon of whisky to put the fire out. When I heard this I went out and joined the brave firemen. I got home all right about one o'clock in the morning, and, as I expected, I found the little lady waiting for me with something to say on her mind. But I pointed to our sleeping child.

"Would'st disturb her innocent slumbers?" I asked. She saw the point and we went peacefully to bed. By morning her good nature had returned, and she passed it all off by merely laughing at me. That's the beauty of the little lady — and not the only kind of beauty she has, either.

5

A BRILLIANT SCHEME.

IF any man wants to make a fortune let him come to Milkville and be a washer-woman — that is, provided he can wash winter underclothes without shrinking them. There is only one woman in Milk-ville who will wash clothes, and she does not care a continental whether she shrinks or doesn't. She's not a shrinking old maid, by a long shot. She shrinks an ordinary suit of underwear just one size at a wash. If she gets hold of a particularly good suit she shrinks them just double that. It caused all the men in town a lot of trouble last year, but this year we worked a scheme on her that was worthy of a Talleyrand. As I am the largest man in town I wear a suit first. Then it is sent to the wash and when it comes back I turn it over to Job Hedson, who is the next largest man. He in turn sends it to the wash and turns it over to Sam Thompson, and so it goes though the village until it gets to little Bill Clarkson, the smallest man in town. After that it is turned over to the children, who wear it in turn, according to size, and eventually it clothes the children's dolls.

There are only two things wrong with this scheme.

One is that little Bill Clarkson won't begin to wear his winter underclothes until next July, and the other is that I have to pay for all of them. But we don't any of us have to wear garments several sizes smaller than our skins. That's a comfort.

The Fooling Of The Fools

I WRITE of an incident of midwinter vacation. There are two youths of this town who are at present inhabiting temporarily larger or smaller portions of the ancient town of Cambridge, Mass. They are the sons of the two wealthiest men in Milkville and are attending Harvard College. Just now they are home on a visit. Naturally enough, Milkville is pretty small potatoes in their eyes, and the inhabitants thereof have but one use on earth, namely to be the butt of their jokes. We held an indignation meeting in our house one day during their visit and decided to either tar and feather these two youths or hang them to the nearest lamp-post. And we would have done it, too, had it not been for Puss.

I will explain that Puss is a very pretty young lady who is visiting us. She is as nice as she is pretty and as clever as she is nice. And she lives in a town considerably larger than Cambridge. When Puss heard of our angry determination she begged us to let her try her hand at taming them, before we resorted to such extreme measures. We agreed, and she asked me to get up a straw ride and have a little supper at our house afterward. Of course, I agreed, and it was further ordered that a number of our neighbors who did not care to take the ride should meet us at the house on our return.

Now these two youths were more than smitten with Puss, which was their only symptom of sanity. In fact, if they had been given the slightest encouragement they would have been tagging around after her all the time. But on the occasion of this straw ride they got their first encouragement. They both desired to be her cavalier and had a quarrel over the matter, which Puss eventually arranged by agreeing to give an arm to each of them. So on the ride they sat on either side of Puss, glared at each other and smiled soulfully on Puss. And the latter kept up an incessant giggling with both of them. I was rather disappointed at this. And I was madder than a wet hen when I discovered by the light of a bonfire at Curd Corners that one of them had his hand in Puss' muff. I was sitting on the front seat with the driver and did not look around again. In fact I fear I swore a little — bitterly but softly — to myself. I did not know what Puss meant by such an action — and I prefer to attend to all such matters myself in my family.

I found out, though, what Puss' scheme was when we alighted and strode up the walk to our front door. The door was open and the house was brilliantly lighted. The little lady was standing in the door and grouped around her were all our neighbors. They were all on the broad grin. Up we walked, headed by Puss and her two faithful cavaliers, and just as the latter got to the edge of the light that streamed from the front door Puss stepped suddenly back with a triumphant little burst of laughter, exposing our two youths each with a hand in her muff. They had been squeezing each other's hands for two mortal hours. It is hardly necessary to add that the young gentlemen from Harvard were suddenly called back to the ancient city of Cambridge, but not until the whole town had laughed them into humility.

As for Puss, I could hug that girl — but I guess I'd better not. I don't want to get my hand into her muff.

THE SIXTH SENSE.

I AM a great be-
liever in the
sixth sense, the
subliminal cons-
ciousness, as they
call it. And I have
become quite an
adept, a n expert
almost at reading
thought.

My wife need
not tell me that
she is displeased
with the letter I
have received from
one of my chums
of the old Bohe-
mian world that I
have forsaken.
There is anger in
the air. I can tell
the state of mind
she is in by her
very step upon the
stair. And when

she enters with a pair of tongs in her hand, picks up the said letter in the said tongs and carries it away to be burned up I know just what she thinks, although she has not said a word.

Yesterday I astonished a friend of mine by telling him that he had just taken a drink. That was mind reading for you. He had eaten a clove, so I could not possibly have smelled the alcohol on his breath. He regarded me with much awe and proposed having another. I did not accept because the little lady has a subliminal consciousness of her own.

I had another proof of this wonderful power only yesterday. A friend of mine called, and I knew that he wanted to borrow money just by the way he turned his X rays on my pocketbook. Is it not truly wonderful and useful, too? In this case it enabled me to get a lie all ready for him and to deliver it with utter *sang froid*. I hate to tell a poor lie — a lame, halting apology for a lie that dare not hold its head up in the company of any other respectable lie it may chance to meet.

"Have I had any experience with thought reading at a distance?" you ask. Indeed

I have, I know a man hundreds of miles from here whose bill I have not yet settled. I know that he is angry with me — quite angry. And yet I have had no communication with him whatever; I have not even written to him.

My Cooking Class.

MY COOKING CLASS.

I HAVE but one student in my cooking class. She would not attend if she did not have to. She is my wife.

My mother was a superior cook as well as housekeeper and, of course, I absorbed a good deal of knowledge about cooking and housekeeping in my earlier years, from her. This I endeavor to impart to my wife from time to time to aid her in her own domestic economy. Do not imagine that I am a fault finder. Far from that, I call myself rather an improvement finder. My wife once said that it was truly wonderful what a number of things I could find in this world to improve. When I was courting her I used to wonder what she could find to love in me, but I know a number of things now. Now I merely ask "How could she help it?"

I started my cooking class when we first began housekeeping and have kept it up ever since. I love to help the little lady, as she tries to improve her cooking, and find many opportunities to assist her by well directed criticism. There is no doubt about it; I am a born critic. If I ever conclude to seek steady employment it will be as a critic.

I had an opportunity to give my wife a lesson in doing one's best under adverse circumstances the other day. There was something wrong with the stove, I believe, and the consequence was a very poor meal after a good deal of exceptionally hard work. I told her about a meal I cooked out West over a campfire. I had an uncle out in the Rockies, and there was a round-up of cattle at a point near his ranch. My uncle had agreed to provide the noonday meal for the fifty men who took part in it. My uncle never did things by halves. That was too large a fraction. He went in for eighths and sixteenths and that sort of thing. I was detailed by him to do the cooking. When the time came to cook I found that our single pack mule had been loaded with a sack of flour, a can of baking powder, a bag of tea and a teapot. Nothing to cook with but the tea pot. Nothing to eat but bread made without salt. Required a dinner for fifty men. I opened the flour sack and made an indention in the centre. Then I poured into it a small quantity of the baking powder. I sifted the baking powder around a little, poured in some water and mixed up some dough. The dough was too watery on one side and too floury on the other, but it had to go. Then I cut a sapling and peeled the bark off. That gave me a good, clean surface. I stuck the dough on the sapling, making a sort of cylindrical loaf. Then I held it over the fire and by constantly turning it eventually got a small loaf of tasteless bread cooked. This I repeated many times. The fifty men came in detachments of ten to eat. Each man got a loaf of bread and they took turns drinking tea by means of the baking powder can.

I explained to my wife that that was all I needed to cook a meal for fifty men. I pointed out to her that there were but four in our family and that the baby was still a bottle baby. So she only had to cook for three. Then I left her to meditate.

But she got even with me. She got me to promise to cook one meal for her. She agreed to get everything ready. When the meal was to be prepared I found that she had provided me with a sack of flour, a can of baking powder, some tea, a tea pot, and a fire in the back yard. I don't think that she meant to intimate that she did not believe me. But after I had spoilt the flour, the baking powder, the tea and a suit of clothes, and nearly set the house on fire, I agreed to stop my cooking class if she would cook that meal.

ELECTION BETS IN OUR TOWN.

THE minister was the only man in our town who did not bet on the election, and he wanted to. There was no money put up. We haven't got much money out in the country, but we bet, nevertheless.

Si Tompkins has rather the hardest time of it. He agreed to kiss his maid-of-all-work every day for three months if he lost. The maid said she would break his head for him if he ever tried. His wife heard of the affair and threatens to get a divorce if he does· And the maid's beau is going to shoot him on sight if he succeeds. Si has to treat eight Republicans every time he fails, and he has a hard winter before him.

Our postmaster has agreed to stop reading postal cards before delivering them. But as he won't be postmaster long, in all probability, he gets off easy. Ben Jackson has got to saw all of Peleg Smith's wood this winter. Dan Green has got to wear his pants hind side 'fore for three months. I have got to wheel the schoolma'am (he's a male schoolma'am) in a wheelbarrow three times daily around the village square, which will be rather hard on me when the snow is four feet deep. But the worst of it is I have got to get up cold winter mornings and build the fires. I don't think the little lady made a square bet on that. If she hadn't bet she would have had to do it anyway, so she had nothing to lose and everything to gain. I am going to argue this point with her, and see if I can't work on her feelings. It's a cruel and unusual punishment, and as such is prohibited by the Constitution.

EXPLAINING THINGS TO A SMALL BOY.

HE is a trifle over three years old. That will explain the matter to a great many people who have had children. To others I will say that it usually proceeds like this, though many and various are the manifestations of his curiosity.

THE BOY — Pop, why do I like to eat more than you do?

MYSELF — Because you are growing more than I am.

THE BOY — Why am I growing more than you are?

MYSELF — Because you are younger than I am.

THE BOY — Why am I younger than you are?

MYSELF — O, let up. Go and play.

(Silence for a few moments.)

THE BOY — Say, Pop, why do women wear different clothes from men?

MYSELF — Because they have to.

THE BOY — Why —

MYSELF — I thought you were going to play.

6   [81]

(Silence for a few more moments.)

THE BOY — Say, Pop, why can't we walk on our hands and feet like dogs and horses?

MYSELF — I don't know.

THE BOY — Are dogs better than men?

MYSELF — Very much — especially better than the grocer who has sent in his bill.

THE BOY — Does God like people better than he does dogs and horses?

MYSELF — No.

THE BOY — Why not?

MYSELF — O, go and ask mamma.

THE BOY — Mamma says you know lots more than than she does, and to ask you things.

MYSELF — She does, eh?

THE BOY — Yes, sir.

MYSELF — Well, I'll buy you five cents worth of candy if you'll go to mamma and ask her questions, one right after another, from now until supper-time. Do you think you can get up enough questions?

THE BOY (*marching off on his errand of mercy*) — Just as easy!

MYSELF (*to myself*) — I am temporarily saved, but he has a smart mother and I fear her next move.

IS THIS IT?

WILL somebody please tell me what "it" is?

I am a parent to a small boy who is educating himself. His method is the direct opposite of that usually followed in schools. Instead of answering questions he asks them. I pass (or fail to pass) an examination at each meal. I usually fail.

My present difficulty is with "it." That boy discovered the other day that "it" rains. That didn't bother him very much. But when "it" snowed a couple of weeks later, he wanted to know who that versatile individual "it" was.   He had me.

He became more mystified than ever when he learned that "it" hailed, that "it" froze, that "it" also thawed, and that "it" was time.   Mystification grew into wonder when he found that "it" was day and also night, that "it" was moonlight and that "it" was noon.   He gave up in despair when he discovered that "it" could grow warmer or colder.

And I shall give up in despair unless some one reconstructs this English language of ours and abolishes "it" altogether.

HOW I BEFRIENDED WILLIAM.

WILLIAM, or Bill, as I prefer to call him, is a favorite of mine. He is a frank, honest-eyed, reckless, energetic youngster, who is always getting into trouble. He has had more escapes from death than any other six boys in the town, and is either being saved for some great use in the world, or to be a horrible example to his fellow-men.

His brother Clifford is quite a different boy. "Kulliford,"as his mother calls him, will some day be a bank cashier, and will depart hurriedly for Canada, in due course of time. If there is an open dare-devil piece of rascality committed in the neighborhood we know that Bill has been around. If there is a mean, sneaking trick played on somebody we are equally sure that "Kulliford" had one or more hands in it. Bill is always found out; "Kulliford" never is. The result is that Bill is lathered about once a day by his loving popper, and "Kulliford" accumulates many merit cards in Sunday School. to the great enjoyment of the anointed. According to Bill, his popper has a cold and cruel way about him that makes matters all the worse. "William," his father says, just as the boy is about to eat a piece of cake at supper time, "you will go upstairs to bed immediately after supper. I will be up there to whip you after I have finished reading the paper." Thus is poor Bill robbed of the joy of eating and held in torture of suspense as well as lathered. Such punishments are cruel and unusual. They are, moreover, inflicted in the dark, and Bill does not get half a chance to dodge. And what is far worse, "Kulliford," who

sleeps in the same bed with Bill, is permitted to enjoy his brother's discomfiture.

The other day Bill came to me, as he
often does, for sympathy. His brother had
committed some high crime or misdemeanor
and had convinced his mother that Bill was
the culprit. That meant a lathering that
evening, and an undeserved one too. I had
been thinking over Bill's troubles and this
time I was prepared to help him.

"Bill," said I, "which side of the bed do
you sleep on?"

"On the side away from the wall," he
answered, ruefully. "Pop makes me sleep
there so he won't mistake Cliff for me in
the dark."

"All right," said I, "Now this time we'll
fix Mr. Clifford. I'll invite your father over
to play a game of chess this evening. That
will make the lathering come late, after both
you boys have gone to sleep. Now, after
Clifford has gone to sleep you roll him over
on to your side and get in his place." Bill
gave me a silent pressure of the hand and
a grateful look that made me feel like a
Talleyrand and a Chevalier Bayard made
into one. The boys are about of the same
size and their voices in moments of extreme
pain and anguish are very similar.

That night, after I had beaten their popper at chess and he had departed for home,
I heard the wail of a lathered boy over in
their house, with feelings of great joy.   I
delayed my departure for business the next
morning in order to congratulate Bill.   He
came over early, as I expected, but he was
a sorry looking sight.   And he came over to
get some arnica and vaseline.   It seems that
the scheme worked all right so far as getting
Clifford duly punished was concerned.   But
the trick was discovered.   Bill got about
four times the lathering that Clifford did.
The latter was presented with fifty cents by
his father to cure his wounded feelings, and
he had given the stable boy next door half
of it to thrash Bill, which the stable boy did
at break of day.   Moreover, their mother
was making a cake solely for Clifford, and
Bill was to be punished that night for fighting with the stable boy.

I have advised Bill to become a Sunday-
school boy and a bank cashier, and I am
going out of the Talleyrand-Bayard business.

SOME blooming idiot of a great man once said that if a man could write down all his experiences and thoughts of a single day, it would make the greatest romance ever written. I have had a few flings at romance in my time, and I thought I would try the old fellow's scheme yesterday. This is the result.

EXPERIENCE — Awoke to find it a dull, rainy day.

THOUGHT ——!

EXPERIENCE — Was informed by my wife that it was wash-day.

THOUGHT ——! ——!!

EXPERIENCE — Wash-day breakfast.

THOUGHT ——! ——!! ——!!!

EXPERIENCE — Baby sick, go for doctor, stay home all day and take care of said baby, wife being busy watching washwoman.

THOUGHT ——! ——!! ——!!! ——!!!!

EXPERIENCE — Wife quarreled with washwoman, discharged her, undertook to finish the job, had to help wife.

THOUGHT ——! ——!! ——!!! ——!!!! ——!!!!!

EXPERIENCE — Quarreled with wife.

[89]

THOUGHT ——! ——!! ——!!! ——!!!!
——!!!!! ——!!!!!!

Any experienced married party knows what the rest of the day was.

Is there any romance in that?

Can anyone discover any poetry floating through that record?

Does it look like a song without words?

Is it even second cousin to humor?

No, it isn't even melodrama.

The only description of art it resembles is the continuous performance.

HOW CAP WENT TO THE WEDDING.

I DON'T like to kick too often about things that go wrong, but there are times I've simply got to think out loud. This time it's about my yellow dog. His name is Cap, and he's a terrier both metaphorically and literally. He hasn't a pedigree as long as that of a certain prince I could name; but he has a whole lot of manly human nature about him. He has his failings, but with all his faults I love him still.

He did not cost me anything *per se*. My wife wanted to name him Percy on that account, but when I recovered she apologized and offered to pay the doctor's bill out of her pin money. But he has cost me a whole lot, nevertheless. I have paid three times for every chicken that was ever raised in our town. In fact they have got to the point now where they import the decapitated parts of deceased fowls from other villages, bamboozle Cap with a caress, stick some feathers to his chin whiskers with mucilage and come around and get fifty cents from me without having to borrow it. The last thing I paid for was a new pair of seventeen button white kid gloves. They belonged to a young lady friend of ours whom we call Puss, and now I've got to my story.

A couple of our neighbors, male and female, young and inexperienced, thought they would like to try the bicycle-built-for-two business, so they got married the other day. I had a sort of prescience that Cap considered himself included in the invitation. He went around most of the time with an amused squint in his left eye. So, ere we started, I locked him in the attic. I don't know how he got out and I don't want to know. It has kept me awake nights wondering for almost a week, and I am trying to get my mind off the subject. But my

wife and I were just looking our level best,
and I was just beginning to think rather
sentimentally of a similar experience we had
gone through some years before, when Cap
walked up the aisle inquiring for the usher.
I cut him as he passed me. I've been
ashamed of it since. I like to stick by my
friends, and he has been a faithful friend to
me. But there are times when I am weak
and yield easily. Besides, I could see pretty
Mrs. Brown, across the aisle, biting her lip
to keep from laughing, and I could tell by
the snickering behind that the rest of them
weren't even biting their lips.

Not finding the usher (and the usher not
being able to find him when he grabbed for
him), Cap went right up on the stage. He
sniffed disparagingly at the bride's train,
took his pound of flesh out of the groom's
ankle and coiled up on the superfluous part of
the minister's robe. Here he would have
remained, no doubt, and caused no further
trouble, had it not been for the organist.
Our organist likes Wagner. His ear has
been educated up to it. My ear is becoming
educated up to it. But Cap's ear is a hundred million years behind the times. He
objects to Wagner and he objects eloquently.
Possibly you may have met a dog in your

experience that objected to music or loved it not wisely but too well. That was what happened.

I thank Heaven and all the saints, however, that my agony did not last as long as it might have. Cap got restless with the first strain from that fugue and he wandered within reach of pretty Puss. He had just begun his solo when she grabbed him and held his yellow jaws together till the end of the ceremony. Oh, I admire that girl!

He ruined her gloves, but I got her a new pair gladly. I would not kick at that, but the boys made me buy too many cigars and things for the safe preservation of the autonomy of my bank account, and ruin is staring me in the face.

I have, however, mapped out a plan of action for the future. The next time two of our youngsters want to commit matrimony I am going to take that dog up to the post-office and lock him in the postmaster's burglar proof safe and stand outside on guard with a shot gun, from the time the first bridesmaid begins doing up her hair till the last shoe is fired at the retreating victims.

HOW I LEARNED TO RIDE THE BIKE.

THE only help I got in learning to ride the bike was from my wife. The little lady would grab hold of the framework just over the rear wheel and maintain my two hundred pounds of peerless manhood while I talked to her and told her what to do, and remonstrated with her for not doing what I thought she ought to do. I do not believe any one else could have helped me as much as she did. You see, I could hardly have talked as freely to any one else.

The last time she helped me my conversation ran something like this:

"Now give me a good start. Hang on! Hold up! Great Scott! are you trying to run me into the ditch! Jane, pay attention to what you're doing. You'll kill me. Don't let me wabble so. Look out, I'm running into a rock, can't you see I am? There! I told you I would. It was all your fault. I should think you would have some sense by this time."

I did not stop here, but I have to make a break in the report of my remarks to say that just here a young lady of whom I am rather fond, in a paternal sort of way, and whom I familiarly call "Puss," rode up on her own wheel and went along with me, although some few yards away for safety's sake. I did not stop talking to the little lady, though. By this time I was too mad to care for appearances. So I turned to Puss and continued:

"Did you ever see such a fool woman? Why can't she hold this blamed thing straight? Here I am wabbling around like a drunken man."

Puss merely grinned and showed her pretty teeth, and gurgled a delightful little girlish laugh. That made me all the madder, and I began at my wife again.

"Now, Jane, do use some sense. Hang on. Put some muscle in it. How would you like it if I let you skin around like this when you were learning. Look out! Ouch! I'm going over. No, I ain't. Yes, I am. Push! Pull! Move the blamed thing along. Stop her — stop her! Can't you see, you great — great — goose, that I'm running in to the fence? I'll be killed! My bicycle will be smashed to pieces. Stop me! I'm gone up! O-o-o-o-o-o-o-o-o-o-o-h!"

And crash! bang! I went into the fence,

just as I had predicted. I picked myself
up and, after an examination, found that no
bones were broken. Then I examined my
wheel and found that it was all right. Then
I looked around to find my wife and give
her a piece of my mind. There she was,
three blocks up the street, just at the point
where I had started, sitting on the curb-
stone and laughing so loud I could hear
every "Ha, ha!" And worse and more of
it, Puss was immediately across the street,
dismounted, and also sitting on the curb-
stone and laughing just as hard.

Then I saw it all. I had made the whole
distance all alone by myself — and I had
been talking, directing and protesting to the
circumambient air. No wonder the girls
laughed. But I forgave them. I had
learned to ride the bike.

7

How We Photographed the Baby.

HOW WE PHOTOGRAPHED THE BABY.

THE photographer fastened the baby in a suspicious-looking mechanism which he averred would hold the baby comfortably and at the same time be invisible (I could not help thinking what an admirable wife and mother such a machine would make), then stepped back and looked inside the camera to see if its insides were all right. Failing to discover a fit of indigestion or other weakness in the machine he shook himself free from the mantle of cloth, stepped to one side, ran his fingers through his hair, grabbed the rubber vermiform appendix that opens the eye of the instrument and remarked in a weary sort of way, as though he anticipated a struggle: "Now look pleasant, please."

I gazed at him pityingly. No need to ask that man whether he was married and the father of children.

"You don't suppose that baby understands such language as that, do you?" said my wife witheringly.

"I always thought I spoke fairly good English," the photographer answered. "However, perhaps the baby will understand you better."

"Well, I should hope so," answered the little lady. Then she smiled upon our infant and said: "Didn't its cutesy wootsey litley bitsey soulsum moulsum want to smilesy wilesy sumsum wumsum for its momsum womsum?"

Our heir apparent gave one look of disgust, curled the northeast corner of her mouth up into her southwest ear, closed her eyes, turned red and yelled bloody murder in choicest baby talk.

"Doesn't seem to work any better than mine, does it?" said the photographer with a sneer.

"Humph!" ejaculated the little lady. "She's afraid of you — and no wonder."

Then the photographer tried again. He put a pet cat on top of the camera and a canary bird on the chair beside it. Then he stirred up a sleepy monkey that reposed in a corner, wound up a mechanical bug and started it across the floor, tooted on a tin horn, and danced a jig. No use. The baby simply looked more disgusted still, and yelled the louder.

Then the little lady sang a song, but without effect. Perceiving that a variety show was in order I took a turn then, and rendered my inimitable imitation of a man trying to recite a poem. Then the photographer performed some clever juggling tricks, the most wonderful of which was extracting two dollars on account from my own pocket (I had hoped to get the photographs charged), and the little lady followed with "Curfew Shall Not Ring To-night." On this I made an impromptu parody entitled "Baby Will Not Smile To-day," and then the little lady suggested that we give her the legitimate. We did. First we gave the dagger scene from "Macbeth," then the sword scene from "Richard III." We closed with Antony's oration, with the little lady as *Antony*, myself as the populace, and the photographer as the corpse. He said he felt like one. The baby "lent us her ears" all right, but look pleasant she would not. Every alternative having failed, I at length resolved upon what I call my "last resort." I got down on my hands and knees and let the youngster toy with my hair and mustache. And then she smiled.

Our friends say it is a splendid picture of the baby, but an awfully poor one of me.

A N insurance agent dropped in upon us one day last week and I fell. I have been tempted before and resisted, but I am getting weak in my old age and am beginning to yield easily.

"Think of them," said the wily agent, pointing to my wife and youngsters, who entered the room at this inopportune moment. I was thinking of them that morning and wondering how I was going to keep a roof over their heads, for the rent was due, and I was figuring out where I could "borrow the price," to use an expression that will be understood in New York. Then reason got to work on me. When reason gets hold of me I am gone. I am not logical enough to battle with it.

"Of what use will be a mere roof," argued Reason, "should you die? They have got to have something to eat and something to wear, and it is dour duty to provide. Besides, you might just as well borrow $200 as $50."

"Oh," said I, making a last futile effort, "my wife is so good looking she'll have no difficulty in marrying again in case I die." At which the little lady looked at me so reproachfully and whisked out of the room so angrily that I was smitten unto the heart. The agent saw my condition and knew that I was his prey.

"I have seven hundred and eighty-four different schemes of insurance and you can take your choice," said he.

I coaxed the little lady  back into the room, and she and I and the agent spent the rest of the day talking over the matter. As a result, when the shades of even fell upon our domicile and the agent had gone up to the tavern to get a drink, I held in my hand the

Mutual Love Company's policy number 131,313,131,313, on my life, and was wondering how soon I was going to die.

It was a queer policy, and about the only thing I was certain of under it was that some day I would die and on that same day the little lady and the youngsters would get something ranging from a capital prize of $10,000 cash down to funeral expenses, which should include a handsome casket with nickel-plated trimmings, a "Gates Ajar" made out of immortelles, and a pillow of flowers on which should appear the legend "Here He Lies." My wife did not exactly like that legend, but I assured her that all my friends and acquaintances would think it appropriate, so it was adopted, with the proviso that it could be changed in case I was blown into minute atoms by some explosion and the services were held by proxy, as it were.

The capital prize of $10,000 was to be paid in case I died decently in my bed at an advanced age. Kind as the insurance companies are. I learn that they have to make a fortune or two out of what one pays in before they are willing to give very much back.

The minimum prize is to be paid in case

of death within one year by accident and in case I am guilty of contributory neglect.

If I am killed on a railroad train or trolley car my widow is to receive $5,000 cash and $10 per week all the rest of her life. If, however, I am killed on a New York cable car she is to receive nothing, but is to pay the insurance company $10,000 as liquidated damages for insuring a born fool.

If I am blown up by dynamite or dropped down by an office-building elevator she is to receive $2,000 cash, a cottage and lot in New Jersey (poor girl), $3 a week, and 100 two-cent stamps, $150 credit at a grocer's, a black dress, a white skirt, one and a half pairs of gloves, a suit of underclothes and a pair of corsets per year.

If I am slain by my fellow-man or gored to death by a bull she is to receive the same as above except that the cottage and lot is to be on Long Island instead of New Jersey, and she is to receive shoes instead of gloves. I do not know which is the more fun, but of the two I prefer the man or bull to the dynamite or elevator — as in the case of the man or bull the little lady will only have to go barehanded, whereas in the case of the dynamite or elevator she will have to go barefooted.

If I slip on a banana peel or am butted to death by a goat she is to receive $4,000, and board for herself and family in a Brooklyn boarding-house.

If I die of cirrhosis of the liver she is to receive the capital prize and a membership in Sorosis. And if I die of appendicitis she is to move to Chicago.

There are several other "ifs" in this policy of mine, but I will not relate any more of them. We are trying to keep some things in our family secret.

But this insurance policy of mine has changed our family life very greatly. I hardly dare stir out of the house any more, and when I do the little lady's brow becomes clouded with care and anxiety. I am thinking of joining the church.

I GET EVEN WITH THE BOYS

WHEN pretty Puss came to visit us a couple of weeks ago she was just beginning to learn to ride a wheel. She looked stunning in her dark green riding habit, and I had great sport helping her to hang on. The slender waist was hers, but the arm around it was mine, you know, and I enjoyed it immensely. But we did not make much progress, and as my wife was beginning to get jealous I eventually had to invite a young man around to teach Puss.

I picked out the homeliest gawk among the wheelmen of the town, but that invitation was a signal to every blooming bachelor that rode a wheel within ten miles of our house to come around and help. I have since learned that the young scamps of to-day keep tab on every girl who learns to ride and swarm around her. It seems that there is no fun riding with a girl after she has learned to ride. The pleasurable excitement comes in when you have to hold her on the wheel, and whisper words of burning encouragement and direction into her pink little shell-like ear.

It made me very tired when I discovered what sort of a game these young men were working. I spoke to the little lady about the matter and offered to resume Puss' instruction exclusively, but she told me that Puss preferred the young unmarried men, and plenty of them, to one homely old curmudgeon of a married man like me.

Well, matters went from bad to worse, and before long we had more than fifty young men hanging around our front steps every evening, smoking vile cigarettes, while they waited their turn at Puss' waist.

I had to lie awake nights to devise a scheme to get even with those young men. But I have quite an intellect when once it gets to work, and eventually I hit upon a plan that was at once cheap and efficacious. I purchased a small brad awl — one so small that

I could easily hide it in the palm of my hand. With this I punched a hole every evening in the tire of one of Puss' wheels. The first youth who arrived after supper of course had to patch the wheel up and pump it full of air. During this interesting process I helped by holding the other wheel — and incidentally punched a hole in that one. Then the young man would have to take a turn repairing that. As he did so I punched another hole in the first wheel.

In this manner, in the course of a couple of weeks, I wore out the patience of fifty-five young men, seven married men, four grandfathers, two physicians and a doctor of divinity. I now have Puss all to myself, and she is learning to ride rapidly. I had to buy her some new tires, but that didn't matter. Like all newspaper men and writers, I am rich.

H

ER OBSERVA-
TIONS.

I GOT inter-
ested in
astronomy not
long ago and
bought a good-
sized telescope which
I mounted in the cupola
of our house, and for several
weeks interested myself making
observations of the star-spangled
heavens. In the course of time I got
tired of this pastime, however, and
one evening after I had announced
that I would make no more observations, my wife said she would go up
and make a few observations on her
own account.

She had been up on the roof rather more
than an hour, I fancy, when she came down-
stairs, her face radiant with success.

"Well," I asked, "did you make any observations?"

"Did I?" she replied. "Well, I should guess."

"I suppose you have made some important discoveries," I suggested sarcastically.

"That's just what I have," said she.

"For instance?" I queried.

"Well, Mr. and Mrs. Brown are having an awful row in their dining room."

So that was her way of making observations, was it?

"Anything else?" I asked.

"Yes, Jack Barnstable is out walking with that horrid grass widow Tompkins (you need never invite him here again); Milly Jones must be engaged to Charley Oliver, for they are sitting on her back porch and he has his arm around her waist and is kissing her;" (they live at the other end of town) "old Mr. Skinflint is cutting the grass on his lawn to save twenty-five cents and doing it in the dark so that no one will see him; Mary Marks went down to the post-office and met Joe Harris there and went to walk with him, although her father has forbidden her having anything to do with him; Mrs. Black's washing is still out and it is going to rain; the Swifts have gone over to the Bakers' and are playing cards, although Mrs. Swift told me only yester-day that she would never speak to Mrs. Baker again, and — ''

But I did not listen further.

I have come to the conclusion that a woman is practical in everything.

THE Women Suffragists of our town were calling on my wife, so I got out of the way. I couldn't help overhearing more or less of what they said, however, and if all things they said about men are true I am heartily ashamed of my sex. Positively, I am going to stop associating with the men and trot solely with the girls.

If the women can't vote merely because the men won't let them I think it is downright mean. My wife takes the right view of the situation. She says the women ought to make the men grant them equal rights. And as every man in the world is under the thumb of some woman, with a good many women's thumbs to spare (according to statistics) it seems to me it would be simple enough to do this.

The little lady has a plan for changing the wording of the Constitution which I think is a good one. The Constitution, according to her (I didn't tell her it was the Declaration of Independence), declares that all men are born free and equal. She would move

8   ·

to amend this by inserting the word "babies" for "men." In the first place, as men are babies when they are born it is more appropriate, and in the second place it makes no distinction regarding sex. "All babies are born free and equal." How is that for a patriotic period?

Well, the little lady declared to those women that she knew I would vote for woman suffrage, and that if I did not she wouldn't live with me. So they called me in to see if she was right.

I made the hit of my life with those women. "Ladies," said I, "most certainly do I believe that the freeman's suffrage should be extended to the gentler sex. Every woman should be permitted to vote, twice — once on each ticket. By this means the women will be satisfied, as they will have exercised the royal right of voting. In fact, they will be more than satisfied, as they will be sure to have voted for the winning ticket. And finally, they will not have interfered with the decision made by the men."

What woman can find fault with that proposition?

But the little lady hasn't spoken to me since for some reason or other.

AN EFFORT AT ECONOMY.

WE had a fit of economy last week — only it didn't fit very well. We needed some coal, and the little lady bought nearly a ton, at half price, from some neighbors who were going to move. Then the question arose as to how we were going to move it over to our house. Finally we concluded to borrow a horse and wagon from a neighbor and cart it over in that. I was to do the shoveling and carting evenings, when I was resting.

I nearly broke my back loading that wagon with coal the first time. I need not say the first time, though, for I never loaded it again. The horse ran away the very first time I said "G'lang" to him. He scattered the coal from Milkville to Curd Corners, and he wiped up parts of three New York counties with me.

That effort at economy cost me just $78 when I had paid all the damages.

I am taking lessons in elocution now. You should hear my imitation of a man swearing.

WILL YER?

I WAS making a tour of the Bowery in the company of a friend. We were both looking for local color. We stopped at a typical Bowery saloon and had a drink. We still live. However, we had our lives insured, so it would have made no difference. As we turned, a hulking loafer made toward us with an impudent grin on his face. "Say, boss," said he, "gimme a quarter, will yer?"

We paid no attention to him, and went out. He followed us. On the sidewalk he approached again. "Look here, young fellers," he said, as he came up behind, "if yer don't give me a quarter I'll foller yer all over town."

"If you follow me a block," I answered him, as gruffly as I could, "I'll have you arrested."

"Will yer?" said he.

We journeyed up town and stopped in various places — to get some local color. There are people who call it inspiration, but I call it local color. He followed us, true to his word. Finally I warned him again. I pointed out a policeman and told him I would turn him over to the officer.

"Will yer?" said he.

We crossed town to Broadway. It was a long and a dark walk. I hoped we had shaken him off, but, as we turned up the street, I saw him not a quarter of a block behind. I was beginning to feel annoyed.

"Let him follow," said my friend. "I know the policeman on the next beat. We'll give him a scare."

We met the policeman, as my friend had anticipated.

"Lave him to me," said the copper. We laved him. But we turned around to see the fun. Our defender caught him by the scruff of the neck, shook him, kicked him a couple of dozen times, threw him half way across the street and chased him a block or so across town. We congratulated ourselves and went on our way.

"If that fellow ever crosses my pathway again," said I, "I'll have him locked up for sure."

"Will yer?" said a familiar voice at my elbow. It was our hulking enemy.

"Look here," I cried angrily, "if you follow me another step I'll break this cane over your head."

"Will yer?" said he with a sneer.

I raised my arm and struck him over the shoulders a terrific blow. He squirmed, but all he said was "Will yer?"

"Let that be a lesson to you," I said. "Next time I'll hit you on the head, as sure as I'm standing here."

"Will yer?" said he.

Human endurance will stand just so much. That settled it. I — gave him the quarter, and invited him into a place where they sell local color and treated him. Then he left us.

OUR MINISTER'S PRESENT.

OUR town of Milkville comes nearer to having the meanest man alive than any other town, hamlet or Ophelia on this unfortunate earth. I will call him Smith, because his name is not Smith, and by making that statement I shall work myself into the good graces of a large and growing portion of our population.

Smith proposed a collection for the minister's Christmas present. As mover of the proposition he was of course made chairman of the committee and appointed his wife treasurer. Then all the women in town went to work and begged of all the other women contributions to the fund and turned over their collections to Mrs. Smith. In this way my wife was enabled to contribute five separate times. She put her name down on the list of every woman who had done likewise for her until I stopped her. There are some sixty women in the town, and as near as I can figure out the facts every one of them kept contributing to different lists until their husbands stopped them. You see that was part of Smith's scheme. And before he was through he had most of the money in town, and wouldn't tell how much he had because he said he was afraid of burglars. He said he would spend all the money, however, for a beeyoutiful piano lamp, and that the ladies could take it over to the minister on Christmas Eve.

You've probably seen, in the course of your long and otherwise upright career, the advertisement of certain firms that give you a box containing seventy kinds of soap, sufficient to last you for a year — thirty-five that you can use and thirty-five that are only fit to give to the poor, with a piano lamp thrown in (the piano lamp for yourself, of course, and not the poor). Well, Smith had bought one of those boxes of soap, and he sold the piano lamp to himself as chairman for the hundred odd dollars the women collected. And that was the present those women took down to the minister last Christmas Eve.

Of course the women did not know anything about it, but the minister's wife is pretty well up in the ways of the world, and when the spokesman of these fool women had made her address, the minister's wife answered for him (he was, of course, overcome with emotion, as is proper on such occasions):

"We thank you very much," said the minister's wife. "Now we shall have two piano lamps just alike. You see, we bought one of those boxes of soap, too.

When the situation dawned on my little lady's mind she said she could have gone straight through the floor to China.

The women have made Smith resign as Superintendent of the Sunday School and the men are talking of lynching him. But, like all mean men, he will probably escape.

ON THE LOSS OF MY CLOTHES.

I WAS very much delighted the other day when the little lady informed me that our youngster was clothed for the winter. I had put by a little money for that purpose, and now it seemed that that was all velvet. Personally I had concluded to wear old clothes this year. I was going to tell the boys that I had agreed to do so in case Bryan lost. But now I could blow in a little on myself. That relieved me of telling one lie, and gave me a glorious opportunity to tell another, *i. e.*, that I had won quite a little sum on McKinley's election.

Before proceeding to invest I went through my wardrobe to see what I needed most.

The little lady had been before me, however, in going through that wardrobe. It was deceased. There were sufficient remains, however, upon which to investigate, and I held an inquest.

The little lady was first witness. Our boy was her exhibit. My last winter's best suit had been manufactured over into a best suit for him, including an extra pair of pants. Ditto with the second best suit. My evening clothes (which she explained I would not need any more) made a beautiful Sunday suit for him, and she had made over my Prince Albert into a jacket for herself. My overcoat had been made over into an ulster for the boy, and my winter under-clothes were just sufficient to fit him out in that line. I had left for my own use a plug hat, a vest and a couple of pairs of socks, also a kid glove (left hand). According to the law of nations that is not sufficient raiment for a citizen of these United States, and I have either got to blow in my princely fortune of $43.74 on new clothes or go to jail or the bath room.

The little lady was so proud of her ac-complishment that I would have been a brute to complain. So I complimented her, kissed her and spent the rest of the day wondering whether I could get credit at my tailor's.

A little more such economy and I am undone.

AN EXPERIENCE WITH INTUITION.

LOVELY woman, God bless her! is one of the strangest of God's creatures. She is not as strange as man, perhaps, but pretty near it. By many she is considered man's superior, and with no false modesty she considers herself to be such. The majority of men acquire a taste for her sooner or later. It seems that she is first endured, then pitied, then embraced.

The most peculiar thing about woman (barring a few hundred others that are more peculiar) is her sense of intuition. She knows things without having read them or been told them. She does not even guess them. She simply knows them. She can read a whole volume between the lines of a letter. My wife can take an ordinary letter from one of her friends and tell just what time it was written, just what the writer wore at the time (especially whether the dress was new or old, etc.), and many other things. Talk about mind reading! Why, letter reading by a woman of good intelligence is ten times as mysterious. The average woman regards the written words of a letter as absolutely superfluous.   In fact, it was my wife's ability to read between the lines that got me into this trouble.   I will proceed to explain:

I was traveling with a party of friends from St. Paul to Chicago on my way home. Now I am very popular, as I lose readily at poker, and the boys wanted me to stay over a few days at Chicago before I journeyed on to New York.   They argued that they had not seen me for a long time and would like to again.   My recollections of the many times they had ''seen'' me in the dear dead past were only too vivid.   I didn't want to go home broke and so I concocted a scheme to thwart them.

I promised the boys that I would stay over with them in Chicago provided I did not get a telegram when we arrived there urging my immediate presence in New York.   They agreed to this, and I slipped away from them quietly at Milwaukee and sent the following telegram to my wife:

''Wire me be home Friday without fail.''

Now my wife received that telegram and went to work to study it out.   It was a trifle difficult for her to read between the lines, she explained to me afterward, as there was

but one line. Moreover, the telegram was
on paper that was absolutely lacking in any
of my characteristics and the writing was
not mine, but the telegraph operator's. She
did her best, however, and supplied such
words as she thought would be correct.

When we reached Chicago we went
directly to the hotel, and as I registered the
clerk handed me a telegram that had just
arrived for me. I exulted. The boys
crowded around to hear whether I could
stay or not, and one of them even went so
far in his excitement as to take the telegram
from me and read it out aloud. This is
what he read:

"Of course I will be home Friday."

She had twisted that telegram into "Wire
me will you be home Friday without fail;"
and I remained in Chicago until the boys
had seen enough of me to buy each of their
wives a new silk dress.

HAROLD'S POEM.

HAROLD is a friend of ours. Or, perhaps, it would be just as well for me to say that we are friends of Harold's. It has never seemed to us that Harold was a friend of ours since the day he killed our cat with a nigger-shooter and tied a tin pail to our dog's tail to make a Roman holiday. But we're friends of Harold's because his mother is a very sweet little widow who is trying to live and bring up a young-man boy or a young-boy man (whichever you happen to call them) at the same time. Harold, by the way, is at college.

The dear soul (I mean his mother, of course) dropped in to see us the other night. She was radiant. Harold had joined a secret society for mutual improvement. As it was a secret society she did not know very much about it, of course. She would not have Harold betray secrets for the world. She wanted him to be a pure, upright, noble man. Therefore she had not asked him any questions about it. He was also writing poetry. She was glad of that. Oh, if

Harold could only be a poet! I joined her fervently in this wish. We could then have a legal excuse for killing him.

Well, a day or two later, I received a letter from Harold. The important part of it ran something like this:

"Say, I'm High-Muck-a-Muck of a Shindig we've started, and we've got to have some rites. I had to get up a song as my share of the rites, and before I submit it to the committee I want to try it on the dog. What I mean is, l want you to look it over and see if it will do, and suggest improvements here and there. I'll do the same for you some day. I enclose copy."

Here is Harold's song. It is evidently a

DRINKING SONG.

Before we sup, fill up the cup
  And toast the maiden divine,
Who mixed her tears and blushes up,
  And so invented wine.

CHORUS —
  All around the table, boys,
    And give 'em cheer on cheer,
  Till they think the tower of Babel, boys,
    Is being built in here.

She kissed the brim to him, to him
  Who had his arm around her;
He drank until the stars grew dim —
  His thirst it did astound her.

CHORUS — All around, etc.

> The horn, the horn she filled till morn,
>   And stirred it up with laughter;
> That maid invented wine, I've sworn —
>   I'll give the date hereafter.

CHORUS — All around, etc.

I did not make any criticisms. But I have induced his mother to take Harold from college. And if the neighbors do not hang him before the winter is over, the Superintendent of the Sunday School and I are going to try to reform him. If we fail in that, however, we have determined to prosecute him for poetry in the first degree.

9

MY MARE.

I HAVE just bought a mare.
Ten families live in our village, and six of them keep horses. The various members of these six families have said nothing about the mare as yet, for they know I can pass any of them going to church (going around by the church, I mean, of course), or going anywhere else. But the amount of horse wisdom possessed by the heads, tails and bodies of the families that do not keep horses passes belief. Jones is one of them. He keeps a cow. He told me that a cow would have been a better investment. He said a horse wouldn't give me any milk for the baby (we are going to buy a pig and name it Orlando — we have the baby, but we have not yet decided on the name for it). Jones merely had to look at the mare to decide that she kicked, bit and balked. He said he wouldn't trust his family with her across the street. As the street in front of his house extends to the Pacific Ocean, and for that matter, to Japan, in real dry weather, I don't blame him for his lack of confidence.

Brown rides a bicycle (or a bike, rather —
I believe the word "bicycle" is labeled ob-
solete in the latest dictionary). Brown is
young, but he saw a horse once, and he had
no trouble in deciding at a glance that the
mare had a pin hip, several spavins and the
lampers. He said, sententiously (you must
always use the word sententiously when
writing for publication nowadays — either
that or tentatively, but I can't work in tentatively here), that it did not cost anything to
feed a bike. You may observe that this remark of Brown's and that of Jones' about
the milk were startingly original thoughts.

Smith, who is a famous pedestrian, was a
little more considerate. He said the only
thing that was the matter with the mare
was the glanders. I'm rather sorry about
that, though, for he says the glanders is an
incurable disease, and I find that he has told
the truth, according to the ten-dollar horse
doctor book that I have just bought.

The remark that Robinson made about
her, however, I really do not understand.
He remarked (sententiously also) that the
mare would eat her head off inside of a
month. Since he said that I have never
gone to the stable without expecting to see
a headless horse standing in the stall. And

the worst of it is that I can find no reference in the horse doctor book to equine *felo de se*. I have a place picked out for her grave, though, in case she does decapitate herself. It is in the Robinson family lot.

PAINTING OUR HOUSE.

I WAS informed by every one in our village that our landlord was a man of his
word and would do just what he agreed to,
so when I got him to agree to paint our
house and surroundings, I thought I had a
pretty good bargain. "I'll paint everything
around the place that you want me to," said
he, with a suave smile that was only slightly
marred by his prodigious chew of tobacco.
That was where I got left. I should have
made him agree to paint the colors that I
desired. Unfortunately our tastes do not
agree, and that house looks like a chromatic
aberration of a nocturne by Whistler.
When I argued with him, he merely said
that he was painting it the color that it
ought to be. Finally I asked him what
color the leaves of the trees around the place
ought to be. "Green," said he, "as a matter
of course." I have him now painting the
autumn leaves green, as fast as they turn.
I am ahead of one landlord anyway.

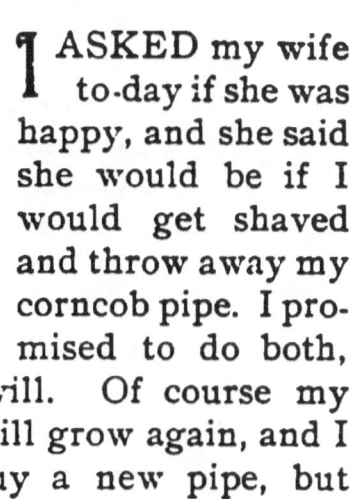

I ASKED my wife to-day if she was happy, and she said she would be if I would get shaved and throw away my corncob pipe. I promised to do both, and I will. Of course my beard will grow again, and I shall buy a new pipe, but that will only give me another opportunity to make her completely happy. You will observe that the things that cause unhappiness are the very ones that give us the opportunity to create happiness. Hence, blessed are the things that cause unhappiness!

I write this for the benefit of young married people. There are people who believe

that I write for the publisher's check that
my writings occasionally bring me — a
check, I may say, that is deftly arranged so
that I cannot raise it the millionth part of a
mill, and bears autographs that I cannot
decipher, much less forge. On the contrary, I write for the edification of those
who have been married just long enough to
discover that matrimony is not "one grand,
sweet song," and that they are separate
human entities, just a wee bit inclined to
scrap once in a while. The adjustment that
takes place at this period of wedded life is
what makes or mars a marriage. Now stop
eating peanuts and listen.

No one would imagine that my wife and I
ever had any differences. But we did at
one period of our lives. Nothing serious,
you know, just a friendly bout of an evening. But they began to worry us, and after
one that was a trifle more serious than the
others (it was about having the dog's ears
cropped, or something as important), we
made up our minds that we simply wouldn't
quarrel any more. But how were we to
arrange it so that we wouldn't? Neither of
us had any memory worth speaking of, and
we had to have some visible means of sup-
port in our determination. Finally, we hit

upon the plan of hanging up a motto that would remind us. Then, when either felt the least bit obstreperous, the other could point to the motto and all would be well. Of course it wouldn't do to choose anything that would be understood by a third party, so we adopted the simple words, "WE WON'T," had them executed in Gothic architecture, framed them and hung them on the wall. I grieve to say that we quarreled as to where to hang our motto, but since the day it was hung peace has reigned in our family.

We had no idea when we put it up how valuable that motto was going to be to us in other ways. In the first place it became a neighborhood mystery. Every one tried to find out what it meant, but of course we couldn't explain. People who had never called on us before called now just to see the motto. In this way it worked us into the best society in town. The effect on book agents and peddlers was marvelous. We always treat such people politely, for we have been poor ourselves — that is, poorer than we are. But we seat them in front of that motto and watch them try to talk. They go out of their own accord and usually forget their samples. And it has a similar effect on charitably inclined ladies who come around begging us to subscribe to African missions and that sort of thing. Even the grocer fell under its influence. He came around one evening to try to get us to pay our bill, looked at the motto, sighed, gave me a cigar, went out and has never bothered us since.

In fact, young people, if you want to be happy, though married, adopt our motto and hang it on your wall.

A COMMUNICATION.

MR. EDITOR:
I wish to know why it is that so many people want to know something or other about the art of dressing, and no one in your valued columns ever asks anything about the art of undressing. Is it moral cowardice? If so, I wish to prove myself a brave man right here and now. I am going to ask the questions for the benefit of mankind and I am going to sign myself "Old Subscriber," "Constant Reader," "Veritas" and all the rest of them, but I shall not go so far as to sign myself Willie Simpkins of West 24th street, which is my true name (the first part of it).

First. I want to know how to get a number five hat off a number seven head at four o'clock of a Sunday morning, after a pleasant and enjoyable evening with a college chum.

Second. I want .to know how to get off a pair of new patent leather shoes and silk stockings at 4:10 A. M., when you can't find your feet with your hands or anything else.

Third, I want to know how to get off a tip-top, nobby dress suit, that cost thirty dollars, but looks as good as a hundred dollar one, when you can't tell the arms from the limbs of the other part, and keep pulling down on the wrong parts and up on the other wrong parts, all this at 4:30 A. M.

Fourth. I want to know — but mamma says I'd better not write any more for to-day; so good-bye for the present.

Yours,
Old Subscriber,
Constant Reader,
Veritas, and the rest

THE SUMMER GIRL'S PROVERBS.

A YOUNG man in the hotel is worth ten in the city.

An engagement in time saves nine.

Love is a mocker, and whosoever is deceived thereby is a chump.

Great riches are rather to be chosen than a good name, and silver and gold than loving favor.

Train up a fiancé in the way he should go, and when he is married he will not depart from it.

A wise girl maketh a glad chaperon, but a foolish one hath lots of fun.

He that winketh with the eye meaneth not business, and should not be considered in the chances of matrimony.

AN IMPORTANT DEFINITION.

I HAD been telling the assembled multitude about a dude who sat next to me at the supper table in a Philadelphia hotel once. This dude was talking to another dude, and was telling him of an ailment he possessed.

"The doctah," said the dude, "pwescwibed a teaspoonful of whisky evwy night on going to bed. But it didn't agwee with me and I had to stop taking it."

"Probably made the blooming idiot drunk," said a Chicago man who was crooking his elbow.

"When is a man drunk?" asked the philosopher of the party.

"A man is drunk when he is three sheets in the wind already and takes a couple more to see whether he is or not," answered the old salt.

"In the army," said the lieutenant, "an officer is never drunk unless the commanding officer finds it out."

"In Kentucky," said a tall man whom we called Colonel, "there is no such thing as drunkenness. You can't get drunk on Kentucky whisky — only happy.''

"You are wrong," broke in the philosopher, "I have made the matter a study with a view to correcting the erroneous impression under which our lexicographers labor. Sooner or later you will see my definition in every dictionary in the land. A man, gentlemen, is drunk when he endeavors to light his cigar at the pump. Then and not till then.''

NOT UP WITH SCIENCE.

IT was in 1925. (You will observe that I am inventing a tense here. I call it the Historical Future Past, and have applied for a copyright.) A pale-faced youth with an immense head and a diminutive body sailed rapidly southward from the southern coast of Australia. After a short journey into the Antarctic Ocean he turned a crank, pressed a button and the boat came to rest.

"I am now," he exclaimed exultingly, "at the antipodes of New York. I am as far away from her father as I can get. Here will I cast the die." He drew his electric aërophone from his pocket and called up New York.

"Give me 79,503 Fifth avenue," he said to the young lady who was running things in the eighty-story building the Western Union has just completed. "Give it to me on your quickest electric wave, and please change that Colorado Madura for a Colorado Claro or stop smoking. I can smell it clear here." A moment later a bell rung in the youth's head.

"Ah, is that you Mr. Richfather? I wanted to speak to you about a little matter. I am Theodore Simpkins. You may have heard your daughter speak of me. I wish to marry her. I am poor but not too proud. Don't swear so, please. What did I understand your answer to be?"

At this moment the youth dropped unconscious, and remained so until the Aurora Australasis came along and bathed his head in *eau de cologne*. He revived in time to thank the Aurora. Then he felt a burning desire at his heart. He took out his Roentgen Ray Ready Relief apparatus and examined his heart closely. Seared upon it was this inscription. "Partially Paralyzed by Pepper's Patent Electric Poor Suitor Annihilator, prepared especially for the use of Purse Proud Papas — patent applied for."

"Invented and put on the market since I left New York ten days ago," muttered the youth sadly. "How can a fellow keep up with science in these days! O, how I wish that I lived back in the days when rich fathers could only kick and usually had the gout."

CAMPING OUT.

AND now hath come ye season when ye tired man of ye city doth think of ye woods and ye green hills far away, and of purling brooks and ye speckled brook trout therein — trout, by the way, that he couldn't catch if he tried for a thousand years.

Yes, this same city man has just bought himself a new hunting suit (Heaven knows what he is going to hunt until next fall), and also the latest patent canoe that he has seen advertised in the magazines, likewise a tent that is absolutely waterproof (I'd like to see one; I've camped out four solid years of my life, taken all together, and I never saw or heard of one), and a few million other things. He has also telegraphed for a "noted guide," at from three to five dollars a day, according to how "noted" the guide is; and he is preparing to hie himself into the forest. There he will practice woodcraft as his famous forefathers did. He will carry the boat (he prefers to say canoe) and do all the chores and cook the meals, and the guide will sit around and tell him stories that were written by Adirondack Murray when he was an infant.

That, O Dreamer, is not camping out. The followers of rollicking Robin Hood did not do it that way. Neither do they do it that way in the far West.

I well remember when I was a fifteen-year-old cow-boy in the wilds of Wyoming, years ago, what we used to consider a swell camp. It consisted of a bed, a frying-pan, an iron pot, and sometimes, if we were absolutely luxurious, a Dutch oven. The bed consisted of a worn and dirty saddle-blanket, for a mattress and coverlet: and for our pillow we used our cowboy saddle. The saddle wasn't so bad a pillow, by the way.

The only objection to it was that the coyotes and other hungry beasts used to come and nibble at it while we were asleep. This was no second-rate camp. It was Fifth Avenue style.

I know of one man whose broncho got away from him, who camped out with nothing for a bed but a copy of the *Rocky Mountain News*. Whether he put it under him or over him I have forgotten. But it snowed that night, and he learned one real use for a newspaper anyhow. I have heard of men who had to resort to old letters from their girls in the East for the same purpose.

That, O Sigher for the Woods, is real camping out. Go try it for a while and you will be perfectly willing to live a few more years in your Fifth Avenue mansion, and have a chance to go to Delmonico's occasionally and get a square meal.

A LEAP-YEAR PROPOSAL IN PHILA-DELPHIA.

SHE — 5 P. M. Will —
6 P. M. You —
7 P. M. Be —
8 P. M. Mine?
HE — 9 P. M. This —
10 P. M. Is —
11 P. M. So —
Midnight. Sudden!

[148]

THE PUGILISTS WHO MET;

OR,

A NEW WAY TO GET THEM TOGETHER.

O'DUFFY, champion heavy-weight tongue-lasher.

McCARTHY, champion heavy-weight chin-shooter.

(They are separated by a distance of five thousand miles.)

O'DUFFY — Hello, ye blackguard.

McCARTHY — Is that you O'Duffy? I thought there was a smell of whisky around.

(Each backs off several thousand miles.)

O'DUFFY — Do yez want to fight me, McCarthy?

McCARTHY — For forty thousand dollars and the championship, ye spalpeen.

(Each backs off several thousand miles further.)

O'DUFFY — Make it an even hundred thousand and I'll put ye to sleep in wan round, McCarthy.

McCARTHY — I'll go ye, O'Duffy, and I won't do a thing to ye but kill ye.

(Each backs off five thousand miles more, and they spend the next two years arranging the details, in luxuriant verbiage.)

O'Duffy — Are ye agreed, McCarthy?

McCarthy — I'm tickled to death, O'Duffy.

O'Duffy — That ye will be McCarthy.

McCarthy — 'Twill be at your wake, O'Duffy.

(On this each begins to back away again. They have backed but a few thousand miles when they meet on the other side of the earth. They faint from fright simultane‥ ously. On coming to, each proclaims the other "champion of the world." They swear eternal friendship and agree to buy each other drinks for the rest of their lives.)

HER ADORER — I am young but innocent, sir, and I love her. Why, I followed her from Newport to Bar Harbor, and I would go to the ends of the earth for her.

HER FATHER — Have you ever rescued her from roughs, while she was doing mission work in the slums of the east side?

HER ADORER — Twice.

HER FATHER — Have you a trysting-place in the park with her?

HER ADORER — Of course I have. Hawthorns and lilacs grow there, and she leaves a five-dollar pair of gloves hanging on a branch of one bush or the other, every time we part.

HER FATHER — And what do you do with those gloves — treasure them?

HER ADORER — O, yes — for a time. Then I have them cleaned and sell them. I have to pay my board occasionally, you know.

HER FATHER — Ah! — I don't remember that in any of Mr. Davis's books.

HER ADORER — You should call him Richard Harding Davis, sir. That last name is too awfully common for the chronicler of New York society.

HER FATHER — Yes, but you know I am only a millionaire, and I like to speak that way. It makes me think that I am familiar with him.

HER ADORER — Possibly you may meet him some day. But you must study his works carefully, sir.

HER FATHER — Are you speaking now sententiously or tentatively?

HER ADORER — Neither; according to the dictionary. But those two words should have occurred in our conversation by this time, so we may as well say both.

HER FATHER — You will pardon me here for referring to the immortal original?

HER ADORER — Certainly, sir; and while you do so I will gaze at his photograph and autograph, for inspiration.

HER FATHER — Ah, to be sure! Have you a past, young man?

HER ADORER — I regret to say that I was born without one.

HER FATHER — It is a fatal defect, sir. You cannot have her. There are plenty of young men who are born with a future before them, but my peerless daughter must have one born with a past. I have sworn it!

A NEW CONSTITUTION.

(Especially prepared for the people of the present day.)

PREAMBLE.

We, the bamboozled people of the United States, in order to give the newspapers of our journalocuted country that which they have already usurped, etc., etc. . . . . do ordain and establish this constitution for the United States of America.

ARTICLE I.

Section 1. All legislative powers herein granted shall be vested in the newspapers of the United States.

Section 2. The House of Representatives shall consist of the daily newspapers of the United States.

Section 3. The Senate shall consist of the weekly newspapers of the United States.

ARTICLE II.

Section 1. The executive power shall be vested in the newspaper owner who may be able to direct the affairs of his paper while residing the furthest distance from the United States.

[153]

ARTICLE III.

Section 1. The judicial power of the United States shall be vested in one good magazine and in such inferior magazines as the one good magazine may consider inferior.

ARTICLE IV.

Section 1. Full faith and credit shall be given to everything published in every newspaper in the United States.

Section 2. Every citizen of the United States shall be compelled to buy and read every newspaper published in the United States.

Done in convention, by the unanimous consent of the newspapers of the United States.

In witness whereof I have hereunto declined to subscribe my immortal name.

Saddened Shade of

GEORGE WASHINGTON.

THE REASON.

PENELOPE — So you were not married last June after all?

PERDITA — No.

PENELOPE — But I thought it was all arranged —

PERDITA — It was.

PENELOPE — And that all your parents and your parents' parents and your friends and enemies had agreed to it —

PERDITA (languidly) — They had.

PENELOPE — And that the day was set and the trousseau bought and the invitations issued, the "officiating clergyman," as they say in the newspapers, engaged and all that —

PERDITA — Yes, all that.

PENELOPE — And that above all you loved each other!

PERDITA — O yes, we loved each other. There was no doubt of that.

PENELOPE — Well then, why in the world didn't you get married?

PERDITA — Well the reason was, my dear girl, that it rained. Wasn't it too bad?

LOVE.

ANOTHER DESCRIPTION.

A YOUNG girl has written me asking what love is. Do you think I ought to tell her? Well, I am going to, but publicly, for family reasons.

Mabel:

When chewing gum and ice cream lose their flavor and even matinees are barely attractive enough to warrant your attending; when you develop a sudden interest in church work and frighten your mother into fits by taking an interest in cooking (a sufficient interest to look on and see how it is done); when, from the time "jocund day stands tiptoe on the misty mountain tops" until the last ray of the setting sun kisses the flowers to sleep, you feel a peaceful ecstasy that resembles the sensation you had that time you took a Turkish bath; when your appetite begins to fail, but nevertheless your friends begin to insist that you never before looked so well —

That is love, t—h—a—t is love.

When mamma warns you to be more careful in your conduct than you have heretofore been, and surprises you with several new dresses and a new bonnet; when papa tells you that he doesn't know how he can ever live without you (and your small brother wanders out of the room intimating that he is something of a liar himself, but that somebody else takes the cake) —

That is love, t—h—a—t is love.

When you begin to think of George all day long and to dream of him at night; when you begin to hate every other girl who looks sideways at him, and discover with the same joy with which a man finds a sleeper in his vest pocket that George is real handsome after all, and you do not know what made you once think him so homely; when he comes in the soft gloaming of the summer evening to sit with you while the little stars that peep ever and anon through the perfumed branches of the trees sing a never-ceasing song of happiness; and finally, when George takes you (delicate little 150-pounder that you are) in his lap, and tells you that those dear little hands of yours shall never be blistered with work, or that pure white brow furrowed with care —

That is love, T—H—A—T is love.

And it is also the worst skin game that is being played in this dear land of ours. Beware of it.

AS HEARD BY HER.

HE — Well, did you enjoy the evening?

SHE — Indeed I did. We went to the opera.

HE — What did you hear?

SHE — What did I hear? Well, what didn't I hear! I heard that Nell Vanderdyke is engaged to Tom Browning, and that Jack Rentsarelow and Edith Singleton have quarreled and are not going to be married after all. Then I heard that Mrs. Tenbroke is going to get a divorce from her husband. Pen Peachblow is going to Europe and expects to bag a duke at the very least. Mrs. Thorndyke has been sued by her dressmaker. The Livingstons have a baby. Count Cantukount is not a Count at all —

HE — But —

SHE — Well, don't interrupt me. I thought you wanted to know what I heard?

HE — So I did, but —

SHE — Well, keep still, then. I —

HE — What I meant was: what opera did you hear?

SHE — Oh — well, I'm sure I can't remember. But I saw the name on the programme.

ADVICE TO THE SWEET GIRL GRADUATE.

L IST to me, O girl! Turn those reluctant feet of yours from the muddy place where the brook and river meet and bend your steps in my direction. Bend your ear in my direction also. I want to whisper a word of advice into it. And don't be afraid of my advice. You'll like it.

Now, my dear, I know the subject of your thoughts. I can't say that I've ever been a girl (although I've been very near one many a time), but I can guess your thoughts just the same. You are wondering, as the sad springtime hastens on to jubilant June, whether it will be better to return to your home and take up your old domestic duties (of reading novels during the daytime and sitting out on the front porch with your young man evenings), like the simple, trust-ing girl you were before you were tried and tempered in the crucible of a fashionable boarding school, or whether you will enter the broader field of earnest endeavor along the right line of duty, and by your noble efforts and magnificent example not only elevate the whole race of man, but also put a lace flounce and a pink ribbon around this battered old cynical hulk of the world that will make it look as cute as a twenty-seven-cent pillow sham. Now that's what you're thinking about, isn't it? I knew it. Give me a piece of gum.

Now, my advice is to adopt the latter and nobler course. Gird up your loins, draw your 'prentice blade and plunge into the arena. No, I don't mean the arena, I mean the thickest of the fight. Come to think about it, though, I guess you'd better choose the arena after all. There's usually better walking in arenas. Cry triumphantly "*Sic Itur ad Astra*" and wade in. If you prefer to sic Astra on Itur instead, why do so. But my own opinion is that Itur can lick Astra any day.

Of course you will have to gain your parents' consent. This can be done by pleading or by paralyzing. The latter is preferable. You can readily paralyze the old man by a few references to Euclid. He'll think you're talking about Euclid avenue, Cleveland, and when you disabuse his mind of the error he will cave in. You can approach your mother on Horace. Shoot off some of his poetry to her in his native dialect. She will think it is some young man you met on the train, and when you explain she will capitulate. Strike while the iron is hot — in other words, while she is doing the week's ironing.

Now I advise you to do this for your own best good. This is just what your parents are expecting and they are all prepared for it. Papa's got a lecture all ready for you and mamma is looking lovingly every day at that slipper she used to use with such telling effect in the dear dead days beyond recall. She is prepared to give you a post-graduate course in everyday life that will be worth money to you in the days when you have to mend your husband's socks. And it will be better all around to get through with it all as soon as possible. Savez?

11

WHIST SIGNALS.

PLAYING the King before the Queen — I am married.

Playing the Queen before the King — I love you.

Trumping partner's ace — I do not love you.

Reneging—I am not so big a fool as I look.

Forgetting what is trumps — I am not thinking of you.

Taking a trick with a deuce — May I see you home?

Establishing a long suit — Meet me by moonlight alone.

Playing second hand high — We are observed.

Spilling the cards when shuffling — Is that homely looking man your husband?

Making a slobbering cut — There are others.

Holding over five trumps — I am rich.

Holding over thirteen trumps — I am a gambler.

Taking all the tricks — Follow me and you will wear diamonds.

CHICAGO (A. D. 2094) — Let me see (*takes the skull*). Alas, poor New Yorick. I knew it, Horatio. A city of infinite jest, of most excellent fancy. It hath borne my debts on its back a thousand times. And how abhorred in my imagination it was — for it failed to get the World's Fair! Here were those hotels at which I got something good to eat the few times in my life that I ever did. Where be your Ward Mc's now, your Ollies, your Bourkes and your Chaunceys that were wont to set the table in a roar? Not one now to mark the Isle of Manhattan. The site of New Yorick is but a curiosity of history. To what base uses we may return at last! (*Throws down skull and spends half an hour computing by logarithms the number of stories in the last office building erected in Chicago*).

[163]

" HE has given me my choice!"
The young reporter crammed a wad
of copy paper into his pocket with a gesture
of despair, ran his hand through a head of
hair that had not been cut since last summer
and shook his fist at a door that bore the
legend, "Managing Editor." Then with a
deftness born of long practice he rolled a
cigarette, lit it, buttoned his coat through-
out and started for the elevator.

"I may either go up to Harlem and interview a clergyman who is on trial for
heresy —"

At this point he paused, unbuttoned his
overcoat, and went down into the depths of
his trousers pockets, with a net result of a
quarter of a dollar. "Car fare ten cents —
beer fifteen — lunch nixey," said he in a
sepulchral voice. And then he pondered
deeply.

"Or I may go to Cuba and write a personal interview with General Weyler on the
conduct of the Cuban war."

Here he paused again and looked long and

thoughtfully at the quarter. And again he ruminated, "Lunch five cents — beer twenty."

An hour and a half later he returned to the office with his copy.

Did the young reporter go to Harlem? Nay, one cannot go to Harlem and return and write a column and a half in an hour and a half.

But one can go to Cuba and return and write the same amount in the given time readily. Especially if one has a sandwich and four beers to bear one up in the undertaking.

HOW.

YOU ask me how to get a play acted.

I can tell you to a moral certainty.

In the first place you must write a play that is bound to be a success, and this fact must be apparent to any manager merely from reading it over.

Make it original, startling, witty, intensely interesting, with plenty of action, etc., etc.

Typewrite and have it copyrighted.

Then take it to a manager. Ask him to read it and leave it with him.

After he has had it six months call for it.

Call again two months later. By this time he has been able to give the story and most of the dialogue to some hack writer who under his directions can reproduce it in as good form as it was in the original. You will probably get it back this time. It will be dirty and some of the pages missing where the strongest scenes are, but you can have it re-typewritten.

Now take it to another manager. He will act precisely as the first did, but he will be quicker. Not on your account, but he will

have heard that the first manager is to pro-
duce that particular story under a different
name and he will have to hustle on his own
account. He has as much right to it as the
other manager, hasn't he? Therefore, why
should you kick?

You may burn the play up now and watch
the fun. You have not only got it produced, but doubly produced, and in a month
the managers will be getting out injunctions
against each other.

Lie low now, and play your cards carefully. If you are very, very shrewd and
particularly cautious, perhaps you may be
able to get one or the other of the managers
to give you $5 for testifying in his behalf.
And by testifying you not only make $5,
but you are enabled to decide which of the
hack writers is to be known as the writer of
the play.

THE STERN REALITIES OF WAR.

DRAMATIS PERSONÆ } *A Society Debutante.*
A Plebe Lieutenant in the Army.

Scene :— A deep window-seat; ball-room in the distance.

She (*admiringly*) — You really lead a very dangerous life, then?

He — On my honor, I assure you.

She — Yet you bear no wounds?

He — I am, like a true soldier, too modest to show them. But if you knew, ah —

She — Indeed! It must be terrible, then. And was it dangerous at West Point?

He — Dangerous? Well, I guess it was. There is no experience a young officer has that is more trying that that. Why, all the pretty girls in the country go there to get married, and the engagement is on all along the line. Many a brave fellow has been captured there. And you've got to fight it out on that line if it takes all summer and all winter, too.

She — But in the army proper — it is not so bad there, is it?

He — Not so bad? Ten times worse.

[168]

You just ought to see some of our poor boys trying to dodge their captains' daughters! Eleven-inch shells from rifled guns are not in it with them. There is no service in the world that compares with ours in dangers of that sort. Why, in the European armies they won't let a fellow marry without the government's permission. With us it is different. We are permitted to run all sorts of risks. The wonder to me is that more of our men are not captured.

SHE — Dear me, is it as bad as that in the Eastern posts?

HE — Just as bad. Why, on one occasion, when my left flank was turned, I found myself engaged to twelve different girls, and was about to capitulate, horse, foot and artillery, to the unlucky thirteenth, when the government took pity on me and sent me out to fight Indians. That was all that saved me.

SHE — But can't you get retired?

HE (*sadly*) — No — the fact is, General Miles thinks I'm too tired already.

SHE — Poor fellow!

BAFFLED.

CHAPPIE — Aw there, deah chappie, I hardly expected to find you at the club to-day. What's up?

ALGIE — Everything. I've given up. That's what's the matter.

CHAPPIE — Given up? Good gwacious, deah boy, you don't mean to say that you're going to quit us?

ALGIE — That's just it.

CHAPPIE — Why you've been the greatest monochromic-maniac of us all. What will we do for a leader without the white plume of Navarre and all that sort of thing we used to hear about at college?

ALGIE — Can't help it, I'm done for, old fellah.

CHAPPIE — Why, what do you mean?

ALGIE — Why, just this. Haven't I bought all my clothes in London?

CHAPPIE — Yes, that's English y'know.

ALGIE — And not paid for them.

CHAPPIE — Yes, that's English y'know.

ALGIE — And turned up my trousers, and played golf and yelled for the Valkyrie III,

[170]

and the Cambridge athletes and all that sort of thing?

CHAPPIE — Yes, that was correct English, y'know.

ALGIE — Well just at the end I have come to the limit of my resources.

CHAPPIE — Aw, you don't mean it, deah boy?

ALGIE — I do. I have discovered that I cannot marry a daughter of the Vanderbilts.

CHAPPIE — Poor boy!

ALGIE — Yes — And I've got to remain poor. That's just what's the matter.

THE GRAMMAR OF MATRIMONY.

DEFINITIONS.

NOUN — The name of a man.

PRONOUN — Anything that stands for a man, *e. g.*, dude, octogenarian, etc.

ADJECTIVE — Word that qualifies a man, *e. g.*, rich, poor, handsome, homely, etc.

VERB — There is but one worth considering, *i. e.*, to love. Neg., to love not.

ADVERB — Anything that qualifies "to love," *e. g.*, "madly, passionately, fondly," or "not a little bit."

PREPOSITION — Anything that introduces a noun. N. B. — If the noun introduced is a proper noun, you are under obligations to the preposition. If a common noun, you are not.

CONJUNCTION — "Yes" or "no," as the case may be.

DECLENSIONS.

There are two — proper and improper.

PROPER — Ah no, I do not love you, and I cannot marry you, but I will be a sister to you.

IMPROPER — What, marry you?   Not on your tin-type.   Go chase yourself, young feller.

CONJUGATIONS.

FUTURE — A husband that is to be.

FUTURE PERFECT — A satisfactory husband that is to be.

PRESENT — Your husband of to-day.

IMPERFECT — The husband you are thinking of getting a divorce from.

PAST — The husband who has gone to that bourne from which no traveler returns.

PAST DEFINITE — The husband from whom you have been divorced.

PAST INDEFINITE— The husband who went away ten years ago, and whose present whereabouts are unknown.

NUMBER.

PLURAL — Married.

SINGULAR — Unmarried.

GENDER.

MASCULINE — A man or a woman who wears bloomers.

FEMININE — Woman who wears skirts.

A Commencement de Siècle Wedding.

A COMMENCEMENT DE SIECLE WEDDING.

(DESCRIBED IN A LETTER FROM THE BRIDE.)

PARIS, June 30th, 1906.

My Dearest Lenore:

Here we are in Paris, and for the first time I have a chance to write a few lines to the dear chum of my girlhood days. I suppose you want to know first about my wedding — you naturally would, as under the old system you would have been first bridesmaid. I know you felt badly that you could not be, and worse that you could not even get into the church; but when you remember that even poor papa and mamma could not be afforded standing-room in the church you will feel less harshly toward me, I know. We are all mere creatures in the hands of a giant power, the press, and hereafter no one who is anyone will ever be able to be married in the presence of anybody but reporters. Just think! The church only seats 1,800 people, and there were over 2,500 reporters present, each one struggling to get more information than any of the others.

But to describe the wedding. In the first

place the officiating clergyman was the religious editor of the *Whirled* (an ex-clergyman). We were both anxious to have dear old Doctor Snorer, but it was impossible. The religious editor did very well, though, and was quite clever. He made a shorthand note of the service as he read it and declared as he kissed me that he got a "beat" on all the other papers in the country, and said he hoped his success would advance him from the "religious" to the "sporting" desk. My bridesmaids were lady reporters from the *Discordor, Cribune, Chimes and Distress*, and I was given away by a reporter from the *Whereald*, who represented papa very well, having had an actor "make him up" for the occasion. Mamma was impersonated by a female reporter from the *Philadelphia Hedger*, which they said was appropriate because it was the dearest old womanly paper in the country. She didn't have to be made up. The ushers were reporters from Boston, and the pages were from two papers in San Francisco. Our coachman was a reporter from St. Louis, and the footman one from Baltimore. The rest I believe simply constituted the audience. A number of the papers insisted at first that Jack and I should be impersonated by reporters, but we consulted a lawyer and he declared that such an arrangement might wed the reporters, but certainly would not wed us, so, as a matter of necessity and after much grumbling on their part, we were eventually permitted to be present at our own wedding.

Our bridal party is a quiet one and as exclusive, I suppose, as we could expect. It consists of Jack and myself, and twenty-four traveling correspondents. They leave us alone in our own suite, and in that and that alone we have our own suite way. There were originally twenty-six of them, but two have departed under instructions to work up a divorce between a French Count and his American wife. A sensation drouth is feared, I believe, in the eastern part of the United States, and they are all very much worried about the news crop. Write soon.

Ever lovingly,
LUCY.

P. S. Do try to be a nobody and to marry a nobody, so that some of our set may be able to see an old-fashioned wedding before the custom is forgotten.

12

THE young reporter walked down Park Row with head erect and chest expanded. Ever and anon he cast a look of pitying contempt over and across the way, where Chester Lord and Arthur Brisbane were drawing a measly $20,000 a year for editorial work on their respective papers. I said "young reporter," but I should have said "ex-reporter," for he was now a dramatist — the only American dramatist in the world. Indeed, he was the very one you have heard talked about as "the coming American Dramatist." He had come. The path to glory was spread before his feet and he had more than $2 in his pocket.

How had he achieved it? Ah, he succeeded

where we have all failed, and, like all geniuses, his plan was simplicity itself. He went to a manager and the manager told him the kind of a plot he wanted. By a little manipulation, in fact, he extracted from the manager all the plot that was necessary to his purpose. Then he went to the star and had the star write the speeches he was to make and arrange the scenes he was to appear in. Then he went to the leading lady and did likewise. Ditto with the villain. Even so with the funny man, who furnished all his own gags. And so on with the rest, even to the servant who surreptitiously drinks of his master's wine while the audience is getting seated in the first act, and the chambermaid who dusts the furniture in the second act while the men who have been out getting a clove are reseating themselves. Was the play accepted? Well, say!

FIN DE SIECLE ARITHMETIC.

1. Laura is worth $150,000. Her father is worth $600,000. Her mother is worth $200,000 and several solid gold teeth. How much do I love Laura?

2. If a grocer's scales weigh three ounces short in every pound, will they ever fall from his eyes? Will he die poor? Will he ever be prosecuted in New York?

3. Two pugilists are matched to fight for $40,000 and the championship of the world. One talks at the rate of three thousand words an hour and the other at the rate of two thousand words an hour. When will they fight?

4. Lord Dunraven progressed eastward at a given velocity. As he progressed, his kick against the *Defender* increased directly with the square of the distance. If he made an ass of himself by the time he reached London, what would he have been had he gone to St. Petersburg?

5. If the Democratic party runs Grover Cleveland for a third term, how many ducks will he shoot in the four years succeeding his present term?

WIFE — Ah, I see you have bought a magazine. Pray what is in it?

HUSBAND — Some more about the lives of Napoleon and Lincoln.

WIFE — Well, what else?

HUSBAND — Another hypodermic injection of Howell's passions.

WIFE — And what else?

HUSBAND —More reminiscences of Stevenson.

WIFE — Ah, and what else?

HUSBAND — Another article on modern artists and their work.

WIFE — What else?

HUSBAND — Some poetry that has neither rhyme nor metre, and that you can't understand, illustrated, with a woman standing upside down on a head of cabbage.

WIFE — Why, my dear, you seem to have read the magazine.

HUSBAND — Oh, no, I haven't read one for a long time. But the table of contents has been the same in every one of them for the last ten years, you will remember.

FOOLISH AMBITION OF THE RICH.

WHETHER it is a fad or an ambition I am not able to say, after all. But I have been struck forcibly by the recent attempts of rich men and rich men's sons to make a name in the world. It is absolutely the only characteristic I have in common with them, and that is why it struck me, I suppose. I dearly wish I had their money in common with them and not their ambition. Just fancy dividing up with John Jacob Astor and quarreling over the last five-cent piece! I suppose he would be willing to match me for it, though. But I will promise not to quarrel if he will promise to divide. If that isn't fair, let him make a proposition that he thinks will be. My P. O. address is — *

Now, there is that daughter of a hundred earls who writes novels better than those of us who have to write them for daily sauerkraut. And then there is that young millionaire who wrote a Jules Verne book and then

---

* (Mr. Hall has no false modesty, nor any other kind, but to prevent his being flooded with letters from millionaires we have concluded to omit the address. THE PUBLISHERS.)

invented a sprinkling-cart. Think of de-
scending from Jules Verne to a sprinkling-
cart! Now comes the aforesaid John Jacob
Astor to investigate the secret of the Keeley
motor, as though every one does not know
that the secret is bi-chloride of gold. Don't
put any money in it, John. Or, if you do,
take it out of your share.

Why, the first thing you know we shall
hear of Chauncey Depew inventing a brake
to a bicycle; or of Teddy Roosevelt perfect-
ing a nose improver that will enable police-
men to smell whisky three miles and a half
away (the best of them can only smell
whiskey a block or so now — mark that I say
smell it, not how far they can smell of it), or
possibly of the Duke of Marlborough patent-
ing a perambulator.

CABLE CAR CONDUCT.

STAND on a corner and signal in dignified manner for the car to stop. This may be done by raising the finger or umbrella. Do not swear or gesticulate. It is a waste of energy.

After twenty-eight cars have passed without stopping pursue one of the two following courses:

Offer the gripman a twenty-five cent cigar to stop, or hire a truckman to block the way with his truck.

Having effected a landing on the cable car, lurch forcibly backward as the car starts.

Step on a fat man's foot.

Hit a dude in the eye-glass with your umbrella.

Knock a baby's head off with your elbow.

Lurch heavily forward every time the car stops.

Lurch backward again when it starts again.

If a pretty girl be on board and within reach, grab her around the waist at each of these lurches. If she is sitting down take a seat in her lap.

Repeat the foregoing at the appropriate times.

Upon the arrival of the car at your corner, bribe the conductor to stop if possible. If not, have your wife and children trained to spread and hold a net in front of your house, and as the car passes jump into it.

Get an accident insurance policy for each trip.

AUTUMN.

HOW beautiful is autumn!
   See the leaves, redder than blushing cheeks.
   See them fall.
   See them lost for aye.
   Ah, the clouds!
   The clouds, the flying clouds!
   The clouds with silver linings!
   Observe! They float in the ethereal blue.
   Ah, the young girl!
   She watches the flying clouds.
   Her heart is as light as the clouds.
   Her little feet trip lightly o'er the pavement made clean by Col. Waring.
   Still she watches the clouds.
   Ah, she falls like the red, red leaves!
   She stepped on a banana peel —
   While her soul was lost with the flying clouds in the ethereal blue.
   Hear her cuss!
   It is autumn.

LOVE.

LOVE — A nervous disorder affecting the entire system, and sometimes even the clothes and food of the victim. Peculiar to both sexes of all ages, from childhood to second childhood. Always fatal in age, seldom in youth.

SYMPTOMS — Loss of appetite and interest in mundane affairs. Anxiety as to personal appearance. Longing for flowers and poetry. Sudden affection for children, especially babies that the victim has formerly despised. Demented belief in the absolute perfection of some being of the opposite sex. Vacant expression of the eyes and cerebral cavity. Patient speaks in monosyllables and takes an especial interest in the monosyllable "yes."

TREATMENT — One dose of the monosyllable "no" and good nursing, for males. For females, a new seal-skin sacque, diamonds and a trip to Europe are often efficacious.

Marriage is an absolute specific. But it is so dangerous that it is never used except in extreme cases.

WHAT HE REMEMBERED

OF THE FIRST SHAKESPEAREAN PLAY HE EVER SAW.

GOOD morrow, good my lord
  Marry, and how now?
E'en so, my lord.
The king doth wake to-night, and takes
his rouse.
Keeps wassel, and the swaggering up-
spring reels.
Gad zooks! Is't so?
I'st.
Think it no more!
For Nature, crescent, does not grow
alone,
Its thew, and bulk —
Odds bobs! And even so!

[188]

CONDENSED GUIDE TO POLITENESS.

CONDUCT IN THE STREET.

WHEN three or four ladies are walking together they should maintain an unbroken line across the pavement. In this way they can regulate the velocity of others without interfering with their own conversation.

If a lady and gentleman meet who are but slightly acquainted the lady should wink first. American ladies never courtesy in the street. Neither do they dance a minuet or other dance.

If a lady offer her arm to a gentleman and he refuse it she should not be offended. Men are proverbially queer.

When a stranger offers to carry you over a mud puddle accept with calmness and *savoir faire*. Do not laugh when the next person comes along, slips and falls into it. Merely scream.

If you wish to stop a car (cable or otherwise), put a couple of tons of pig iron on the track. If you have not time to do this take a running jump and get on the best way you can.

A DOMESTIC CONVERSATION.

HER FATHER — So you have had a proposal, my daughter?

HERSELF — Yes, papa — several. An iceman proposed to me.

HER FATHER (*breathlessly*)— Did you accept him, my dear?

HERSELF — Nay, nay, papa.

HER FATHER — Ingrate!

HERSELF — After him a plumber proposed to me, dear papa.

HER FATHER (*excitedly*) — And him — did you accept him?

HERSELF — Not for jewels and precious stones, papa mine.

HER FATHER — Fool! Idiot!

HERSELF — I had a third proposal, papa. The gentleman is an iceman in the summer time and a plumber in the winter.

HER FATHER (*on the verge of apoplexy*) — Madeline —

HERSELF (*calmly*) — I accepted him, father.

HER FATHER — Fall on my neck, my angel child — you are the rarest rose of them all.

[190]

IT IS SPRING.

IT is Spring.
The merry birds sing lustily in the budding trees.

Gentle breezes blow hither and thither in wanton sport.

The sun smiles with lovely radiance on all the green glad land.

Flowers are scattered by the magnificent hand of Providence over all the land; we can buy roses around the corner at the florist's at $8.00 per dozen. Nay, I do not mean that we can buy them, but that he can sell them at that price.

It is Spring, gladsome Spring, and the only drawbacks to our perfect enjoyment of the fact are these:

We are out of a job.

We are out of money.

We are out of credit.

We are out of provisions.

We are out of coal.

We are out at elbows.

We are *not* out of debt.

And we fear that we shall soon be put out of doors.

A LETTER TO HER HUSBAND.

(FIN-DE-SIECLE STYLE.)

DEAR WILL:

Our daughter Ethel was married to a young man seventeen minutes after our arrival at this most delightful of all summer resorts. I have not yet met the young man. May, being two years younger, took almost three hours to secure a husband. Poor dear! she is not nearly so experienced as Ethel, so there is no reason why she should feel so mortified. Our George is not doing nearly as well as the girls. He has proposed eleven times, and tells me he got the "marble heart," whatever that means, in every instance. He has only been here twenty-four hours, however, and in my opinion was handicapped by his bicycle suit. They are so common, you know. Perhaps in his golfing costume, to-morrow, he may do better. The baby is flirting with a pair of twins in the moonlight on the back piazza. That he will marry one of them before the week is out I am quite sure. But I do hope the poor dear will not commit bigamy — or shall I call it littleamy? I will see you when I come down Saturday, if I do not in the meanwhile elope with a young French count who is stopping here. Every one says he is a spurious count. I don't know just what they mean by that, but I suppose it is something very complimentary.

Lovingly, but hastily,
MARIA.

13

CONDENSED GUIDE TO POLITENESS.

THE MAKING OF VISITS.

DON'T visit slight acquaintances for a longer period than a month — if you do, however, do not complain about the food.

If a servant purloin your watch or other valuables do not complain to your hostess. Take one of hers. You stand a good chance of getting the better of the bargain.

It is considered *de trop* in the *haut monde* to use your hostess' carriage more than eight hours a day.

Don't gossip about your hostess until you have concluded your visit. Do not get so interested in her private correspondence as to become preoccupied, unless you are quite sure she will not return unexpectedly.

Do not spank her children for her, or offer to lighten her sorrows by poisoning any of her canines and felines.

While a guest, do not borrow anything but money. You would have to return anything else.

Be blithesome and cheerful. In a word, act as though you were entirely at home, which is equivalent to saying do not act as you do when you are at home.

HOW TO BEHAVE.

NEVER lie — or at least if you must lie lie about something nobody knows or cares about, so you will not be caught. Avoid exaggeration. Every one is "onto it."

Never laugh at the fate of others — excepting only the predicament of the man who, with seven bundles of dry goods for his wife, has fallen into three inches of mud.

Never treat a man to a cock-tail in the expectation that he will treat you to one in turn. On the contrary stand before the bar talking about yourself until he is willing to treat you to shut you up. You are then ahead of the game and can cease talking with dignity and a drink.

Never give your seat in a car to any but a pretty woman. The homely ones all have disagreeable tempers and might not thank you, which would be disappointing, I don't think.

When a man asks you to lend him fifty dollars don't lie to him. Be a man and tell him you haven't it. You can't fool a man who is dead broke.

HINTS ON SWIMMING.

GO to some place where there is sufficient water. There is no use trying to swim in a dew or a heavy mist.

Procure a bathing suit. If you were to bathe in your store clothes or dress suit you would be considered eccentric, and justly so.

Procure an instructor. A pretty girl makes the best instructor for a young man, and a good-looking youth for a young and timid girl.

Enter the water boldly if you are a man — timidly if you are a girl. These are conventional antics. It is safe betting that the girl is more familiar with water than the man, but that doesn't count.

If you are of the male persuasion, remain as close as possible to the side of your fair teacher. If you are of the female persuasion, remain closer.

Remark that "The water is rather wet today," to show that you can be witty and original under the most trying circumstances.

Shriek and yell in order to furnish some excitement for the spectators. It is by such

thoughtfulness as this that we endear ourselves to others.

Now throw out your hands, throw back
your head as though you had the spinal
meningitis, draw up your legs (if a girl I
mean limbs, of course), take a long breath,
it may be your last, and strike out just as
they told you to in that book you were
studying the night before.

Make a bold effort. Kick, struggle,
scream for help, swallow a gallon of water,
and say your prayers hurriedly. Grab your
instructor anywhere, but about the neck
if possible, and hang on tight. Choke him
or her if possible. At all events pull out
some of his or her hair to remember the occasion by.

If you are not drowned thank your instructor kindly for saving your life — a life
that was worthless until that moment, but
which you will now endeavor to make
worthy, etc., etc.

If you are drowned this may be omitted.

THE HERO-MAKER

YOUNG Mr. Morrison of the *Daily Planet* wandered out on one of the numerous piers that make certain fashionable portions of the Atlantic coast look like the rim of a gigantic cogwheel. It was the last day of his vacation and he was getting ready to return to the hot metropolis. He had spent the morning bidding good-bye to three young ladies to whom he had been making violent and simultaneous love. With the savings of a year he had posed for two glorious weeks as a young man of fortune, and, to use his own expression, he had "torn Mt. Desert wide open." He had been looked upon with great favor by the feminine contingent of idlers, but with growing suspicion by the adolescent collegians who associated with them. He had won the hearts of the young ladies and the money of the young gentlemen with equal ease. As he had returned the hearts to the keeping of the young men, however, and spent the money on the young ladies, he could not look upon himself in any other light than that of a public benefactor. Hence he was contemplating himself with considerable satisfaction as he strolled up the pier. There still was the greater part of a hundred dollars in his pocketbook and three locks of hair and a dozen cigars more or less equally distributed through his clothes.

The pier was vacant save for the presence of a solitary little girl who sat on a camp chair at the end of it. He glanced at her quite casually.

"She is clad in raiment as white as the driven snow," said he to himself, with a self-appreciative grin, "and her golden hair is hanging down her back." But as he approached her more closely, he suddenly exclaimed, "By Jove, she's crying!" He walked up to her. She was indeed crying bitterly.

"Hello, kid," said young Mr. Morrison, laying his hand soothingly on her shoulder, "what's the matter?"

"I'm bewailing my fate," whimpered the little girl.

"WHAT'S THE MATTER?"

"Bewailing your fate, eh? Humph! Sounds kind of professional. I say, kid, are your father and mother devotees of Momus,

Terpsichore, or any of those ducks? I mean, are they on the stage?"

"No," answered the little girl, "but they are cruel."

"Ah, worshipers at the shrine of Bacchus, probably," mused Mr. Morrison. "Well, in what particular way are they cruel, kid? Tell me. Perhaps I can do something for you. I'm a sort of a knight-errant, that is, I do most of my work at night and make a good many errors, according to the city editor. But confide in me, nevertheless. Perhaps I can get the *Planet* to take up your case and put you under the protection of the S. P. C. C. In what way are they cruel?"

"They make me earn their living," blubbered the girl.

"Make you earn their living! Well, it can't be much of a living. I don't believe you are a day over ten years of age. What is your particular line?"

"I'm a hero-maker, sir," she answered.

"A hero-maker," gasped the astonished reporter. "Well, that's a new one. Everything is new nowadays — even my cuffs. I suppose you're a 'new' girl' and before long I fancy we'll be hearing of 'new' babies. Will you kindly tell me what a hero-maker is and how you make a living by being one?"

"I permit my life to be saved," said the little girl seriously.

"That's strange," ejaculated Mr. Morrison. "Most people object to familiarities of that description."

"You don't understand," said the girl.

"No, I'm afraid I don't."

"It's this way," she explained. "Lots of people, young men of fortune mostly, but now and then young women who want to make an impression, like to get a reputation as life-savers. Papa talks it up with the young men he thinks will do, and mamma with the young women. Then, if they are willing to pay the fee of fifty dollars, I fall into the water and let them rescue me. Then papa writes them a letter of thanks and gives them a photograph of me with an appropriate inscription on it. It's a great scheme. My life has been saved ever so many times. We go to all the famous ocean resorts in the world."

"Yes, it's a great scheme," assented Mr. Morrison, whistling softly to himself, "but I don't see anything particularly cruel about it." There was a chance for professional work here, and he appreciated the opportunity.

"Well, you would if you were in my place," she went on. "You see, they really

do save my life. I can't swim a stroke, and
if they didn't I'd drown. It's too *bona fide.*
That's what's the matter with it, and I'm
frightened to death every time I fall in."
And, like all women, new and old, she proceeded to prove her terror by her tears.

"That puts a different face on the matter,"
the young man admitted. And he set his
quick wits to work to figure out a plan by
which the *Planet* could rescue this girl from
her cruel parents with due credit to itself
and incidentally to him. Suddenly he heard
a simultaneous crash and shriek and looked
up in time to see the little girl fall backward
into the sea. The rickety little camp stool,
provided no doubt by her cruel parents, had
broken, or rather parted, and precipitated
her into the water. In an instant young
Mr. Morrison followed her. He was a strong
swimmer and in a few minutes had her back
on the pier.

"There," said he, much pleased with himself, "that time your life was saved in dead
earnest."

"Oh, you're so good, so noble," murmured the hero-maker.

Mr. Morrison thought pleasantly of the
paragraph in the *Planet's* statement of the
case in which it referred to the gallant

manner in which one of its own reporters really and legitimately had saved the little girl's life, thereby winning her confidence and learning her cruel secret. The young lady herself was crying harder than ever now.

"There, there," he said, consolingly, "everything's all right. I'll have your mother and father before a court within a week. All you've got to do is to keep from being drowned in the meanwhile. I'd show you something about swimming if I had time, but I have only half an hour left to pack up and take the train. Good-bye — "

" But I shall be beaten and starved!" shrieked the little girl.

"Why?" asked her preserver blankly.

" Because they'll think I've been doing business on my own hook and they'll want the money — and I won't have any to give them."

"That's a fact," assented he. "Hadn't thought of that. I'll fix that all right, though. Here's your fifty dollars and you can tell them you caught a sucker. I'll get even with them later." And Mr. Morrison handed her fifty of his remaining dollars, kissed her and hastened to his hotel.

The next afternoon, in high spirits, young Mr. Morrison of the *Daily Planet* walked into an uptown resort much frequented by his *confrères* on the daily press of New York. Duncan, the free lance and special writer, was there, and was telling, bombastically as was his wont, of a "story" he had just written up and sold to the *Planet*.

"LITTLE GIRL ACT, YOU KNOW."

"It's about some clever English swindlers, Morrison," said Duncan. "One of them is a dwarf (she used to give swimming exhibitions in Europe, by the way) who poses as the daughter (little girl act, you know) of the other two. She appeals to the sympathies of verdant young men by telling them

that she is a hero-maker — that is, her
parents make her fall into the water and be
rescued by young men seeking glory in the
eyes of their sweethearts, at fifty dollars a
head. She is seated, while telling her little
fairy tale, on a trick chair that collapses at
about this point, and in she goes. Of
course Mr. Verdant goes in after her, pulls
her out and thinks himself a big man. Then
she plays the clever part of her game. She
tells him that her parents will think she has
worked the game and will demand the fifty,
with whippings and all that sort of thing if
they don't get it. Of course Mr. Verdant
produces the long green and — why, where
are you going, Morrison?"

"I'm going to the dentist's," answered
that young man, with a look of disgust on
his face. And he added to himself, when he
had reached the street, "to get my eye teeth
cut."

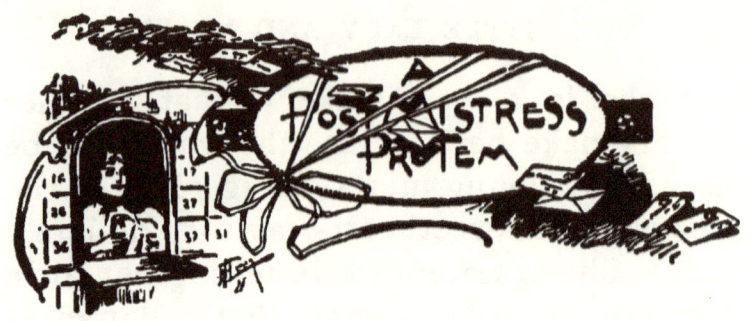

A POSTMISTRESS PRO TEM

I WILL introduce myself as Mr. Frank Wheaton, one of the younger members of the St. Paul bar, and at the period of these events visiting in New York. To be as brief in explanation as possible, my friends had concluded that it was high time for me to be married. My protestations were over-ruled, and although my heart had never experienced the gentle passion for any particular girl, I eventually picked one out from the number of my fair acquaintances, and decided to offer myself to her. Miss Violet Pierson, of New York, was as good as she was beautiful, and was an heiress besides. I arranged with my partner for a short vacation, proceeded to New York, and offered myself, one fine June day, to the young lady, in person. Violet received my proposition with as

much dignity as I had made it, assured me of
her esteem, told me she would consult with
her parents and give me an answer on the
next day. As I had never had the pleasure
of meeting either her father or mother I left
with her a photograph of myself with my
autograph on the back, that they might in
some manner judge of my character. If I
had been pleading the cause of another I
should have marked it "Exhibit A." But
I have always been careless of my own in-
terests, and to tell the truth I was so embar-
rassed during the entire interview that I lost
for a time all my business acuteness.

After leaving Violet's Fifth Avenue home,
I proceeded on my way down town to meet,
for the first time in several years, my old
college chum, Jack Dennett. At Union
Square, I attempted to board a cable car as
it swung around what I know now as Dead
Man's Curve. And then —

Then I awoke in the Presbyterian Hos-
pital, with Jack bending tenderly over my
bed.

"Not a word," said Jack, cautioningly.
"You are not even to think. You had a
severe concussion of the brain, my dear fellow, and nothing but complete rest will get
the contents of that head of yours back into
shape."

"I must see Violet at once," I whispered.

"Drop that," said Jack, authoritatively. "You have been seeing violet and every color of the rainbow ever since you were hurt. Not another word now."

With that he left me. I will not describe the monotonous existence of the next three weeks of my life; but a day came eventually when they put me on the cars destined for a quiet little town in the Adirondacks, where a quiet life, the air of the woods, and absolute rest from all the worry and care of this world were to complete the cure. It was a place recommended by a friend of Jack's who had once been threatened with insanity. He assured Jack that no human being could possibly find anything to think about in that town except sleeping and eating. Hence it was just the place for me. So, off Jack shipped me, clad in a suit of clothes from his own wardrobe (mine had been ruined in the accident) and with linen of all descriptions, from the same place. Jack and I were exact mates in size, so he had not troubled himself to go through my trunk for supplies. And as he said good-by to me the dear fellow shoved seventy-five dollars in bills into my hands, a ticket into the ribbon around my hat, and a long flat parcel done up in brown wrapping paper onto the seat beside me.   He told me to write to him for more money when the seventy-five was

exhausted, and made me promise to look at the contents of the package four times daily — before each meal and on going to bed. Jack said it was his prescription.   By the way, Jack was always peculiar.

That night I slept under the hospitable roof of a cleanly old widow, a Mrs. White, in the little town of L——. I had been enjoined to stay there at least six weeks, so I paid her in advance my board and washing for that time. This left me about $6 in cash, most of which I laid out in cheap novels, tobacco, pipes, writing materials and stamps. And I adorned my room with the contents of the brown paper covered parcel. It proved to be a framed motto, and the mandate on it was "Don't Worry."

I spent the first few days of my stay in writing letters — the first and longest of which, you may be sure, was to Miss Violet Pierson, explaining at length the reason for my failure to call upon her again, and my present condition. And I begged her, of course, to let me know my fate at once by mail. In spite of Jack's motto I was already beginning to worry. On the third day of my stay I went to the little village post-office and asked for letters for Mr. Frank Wheaton. I expected to find in the village postmaster the usual senile old man so common in such places. But framed in the little arched window of that country post-office was the head of a Venus worthy the hand and brush of a Titian. My embarrassment in the presence of Miss Violet Pierson was absolutely insignificant compared with my trepidation in the presence of this auburn-haired, rose-cheeked, star-eyed Postmistress. In a word I was smitten at first sight.

"If this be love," thought I, "I've got it bad, and I've got something more to worry about, too."

"Have you anything by which to identify yourself?" said the pretty Postmistress, with a smile that disclosed two rows of pearly teeth.

"Will old letters do?" I asked, falteringly.

"I guess so," she replied. "But I'm not very well informed, and I have to be careful. You see I'm only Postmistress *pro tem.* This is the way I spend my vacation. It's fun for a city girl, you know, and it gives my uncle, the real Postmaster, a chance to go up in the woods and rest."

"Of course you must be careful," said I, endeavoring to conceal my embarrassment behind a patronizing air. "My mail is of the greatest importance. But these letters will satisfy you as to my identity." With this I drew from the inner pocket of my coat a bunch of old letters and handed them to her. She glanced at them at first curiously. Then she frowned and drew the contents from several of them and read them hurriedly. Finally she spoke.

"I believe you asked for mail for Mr. Frank Wheaton?" said she.

I thought her tone a trifle severe. But I answered: "I did."

"Then I am afraid you are not as honest as you look, Mr. John Dennett," she replied, accenting the name in a manner peculiar to angry woman.

The situation nearly took my breath away. Jack had left some old letters in his pocket. I was wearing his coat, and I had fully identified myself as another person.

"This is an unfortunate mistake," I tried to explain, weakly. "I am wearing a coat belonging to a friend of mine and did not know there were any letters in the pocket. Naturally I —"

"Wearing another man's coat," she mused. "Goodness, I hope you're not a burglar! I must notify our constable the moment I close up the office for the day. That will be very soon, now. If you want to escape you'd better hurry."

I have been in predicaments before and I paid no attention to her — or tried not to.

"Will you be kind enough to tell me whether there are any letters here for Mr.

Frank Wheaton?'' I asked, as coolly as possible.

"O, I don't mind telling you that. In fact I have taken especial interest in them. You see nobody seems to know who he is, and he must be a gentleman, because he has a letter from a lady and the envelope is of the very latest fashion. I'm going to get some of the same kind myself. Besides that, there are several letters from men. Now, you evidently know who he is, or you would not be trying to get his mail. I've done you a favor; will you tell me who he is and where he is living?''

"I am he," I answered.

"Look me straight in the eyes and repeat that," she commanded, very seriously.

"I am he," I repeated, looking straight into the prettiest blue eyes this side of heaven.

"Too bad," she said, with a shake of her head. "Mamma told me once that a man who could look straight in the eyes and could then tell an untruth must be a very bad man."

I turned on my heel and walked out. It was time to swear, and it is a matter of principle with me never to swear before a woman. And I never forget this principle

before a pretty woman.   I went home to my
room and looked at Jack's motto.   I wanted

to smash the mocking thing with my
clenched fist, but I went down to Mrs.
White for consolation instead.   I told her
my story.   This is the consolation I got:

"Young man," said she, "I suspected you from the first. Any man who pays his board six weeks in advance ought to be suspected. Honest men don't have to do that sort of thing. I have no doubt that you are John Dennett. Your clothes are all marked with that name. And you have been trying to steal Mr. Wheaton's letters, poor gentleman! And to think that I should harbor such a rascal under my roof! I ought to put you out in the street, but I need the money and times are hard. One thing I will do, though; I shall put myself under the protection of the constable. He lives next door, and you just try any of your nefarious practices on me if you dare. You can stay here until your board money is worked out, unless they take you to jail in the meanwhile, which I trust and pray they will. But you can't stay with me one minute after your six weeks is up, even if they don't."

I went from her irate presence to my own room and threw a hair brush at Jack's motto. It missed. Then I sought the telegraph office and wrote out a telegram to Jack.

"That don't go through this office," said the telegraph operator. "You're sending

that telegram to yourself and signing it with
another man's name. It's against the rules
to use the wires for criminal operations.
O, we're onto you, young feller!''

I bit my lip and crossed the street to the
cigar store. When I am in a predicament
and am studying my way out, I like to chew
an unlit cigar. The proprietor refused to
sell me one.

"Money's too scarce in this region to take
any risk on counterfeits. I suppose you've
stuck me already, but if you have I'll have
the law of you." I left him and sought the
Postmistress *pro tem.* once more. I resolved
to tell her my story and throw myself on
her womanly mercy. But I learned that she
had gone out walking. There was but one
mail a day, and the post-office closed at 2
P. M. I went to my room after that and
spent the rest of the day swearing at Jack's
motto.

During the following week matters went
from bad to worse. I left the house but
once a day now. The fact is I had become
conspicuous. I went to the post-office once
each day to expostulate with the Postmistress *pro tem.* When I did so grown people
shunned me and little girls ran crying to
their mothers. The small boys of the town,

however, followed me around in a drove.
But I went, nevertheless. The fact is, I
had grown rather fond of expostulating with
the pretty Postmistress. Shall I say that I
had also grown rather fond of the Postmis.
tress herself? Well, perhaps more than fond.
But was a man ever so handicapped in his
courting? She still insisted on calling me
Mr. Dennett. I learned, though, that
another letter had arrived for Mr. Wheaton,
addressed in the same feminine hand, and
many more in business envelopes. But not
one would she deliver to me.

Disgusted at the absurd situation in which
I was placed, and at my own unavailing
efforts to extricate myself from it, I resolved
one afternoon to vary the monotony of my
disagreeable vacation by a walk in the
woods. The course of my wanderings led
me to the foot of a gnarled old tree whose
huge limbs were but six or eight feet from
the ground. I sat down at its base, reclined
against it, and began studying the matter
over. I have the habit of talking to myself
when I am alone.

"Here I am," I mused, "without money
enough to get home, and no possible chance
of getting any unless I renounce my right-
ful name and tell them to send me money,

using the name of Jack Dennett. But do I want to get home? No, not while that auburn-haired Postmistress remains here. Here I am, and I have no idea whether I have been accepted by Miss Violet Pierson or not. But do I want to be accepted by Miss Violet Pierson? Decidedly not. Most assuredly not, if that auburn-haired Postmistress is neither married nor engaged. Now, do I love that auburn-haired Postmistress? I do, most pronouncedly. I love the ground she walks on, the stamps she sells, the pen she writes with, and, if I feel that way toward her I must love her sincerely, for she has got me into the worst mess of trouble I ever experienced in my life. But, under existing circumstances, I cannot even make love to her; I'm blessed if I'll court her under the name of Jack Dennett. Let Jack do his own courting. And she won't recognize me under any other name, nor could I entertain her if she did. I have money enough left to buy her two or three ice creams, but the ice cream man won't sell to me any more than the rest of them will. Of one thing, though, I am certain. I love her, and I am going to marry her if I have to break Violet's heart, and —"

"Keep me up here all the rest of the afternoon listening to your nonsense?"

It was the voice of the Postmistress *pro tem*. I looked up. There she was seated on a low hanging branch of that self-same tree. She had been reading a novel. She

was blushing and laughing. And she was a very picture too.

"I — I — I — beg your pardon," said I.

"Well, I think you ought to," she answered. "But you needn't be so afraid

of breaking Violet's heart if you really are
Mr. Frank Wheaton.   See."   She held up
a large rectangular envelope.   "It is the last
letter for Mr. Wheaton from the girl in New
York," she continued.   "And she is either
sending him her photograph, or she is sending his back to him.   Undoubtedly the
latter, as he has been such a poor corre-
spondent.   Oh!"

The letter dropped at my feet.

"Thank you," said I, tearing it open.
"Do you carry the mail around with you on
your ramblings?"

"I do his mail," she answered, faintly,
"for something told me, the very first day
a letter came for him, that — that I ought to
be particularly careful of his mail.   Perhaps
I feared you would steal it, you know."

"Look," said I, not heeding her.   The
letter contained nothing but the photograph
I had left with Violet as "Exhibit A."   I
handed it up to her.   "Is that identification
enough?"

"It certainly is."

"Permit me to introduce myself, then,"
said I, "Mr. Frank Wheaton, of St. Paul."

"I am Miss Frances Baring, of Albany,"
she replied.   "And what an awful lot of
trouble I've got you into!   Here are the rest

of your letters. I hope you will not report poor dear Uncle Ned."

"You overheard what I said, when I was talking to myself?" I asked.

"Yes, I couldn't help it," she answered.

"Well, do you suppose I would do your uncle any harm under — under those circumstances?" She did not reply for a few moments. Then she said: "Did you think very much of her? Perhaps — perhaps you are engaged to her."

"Look!" said I. I took the bundle of letters and looked through them for the reply from Violet to my first letter. When I found it I held it up before the Postmistress *pro tem.* and tore it, unopened, into small pieces and flung them to the breeze.

"Are you satisfied now?" I asked her.

I am not going to say what her reply was. But I'm glad I didn't smash Jack's motto. It hangs in our parlor to-day.

www.ingramcontent.com/pod-product-compliance
Lightning Source LLC
Chambersburg PA
CBHW030134030726
47498CB00007B/2706